Hotwife for the Seasons

4 Spicy Wife-Sharing Stories

Hotwife for the Summer
Hotwife for the Fall
Hotwife for the Winter
Hotwife for the Spring

Lacey Cross

Contents

HOTWIFE FOR THE SUMMER

A First Time Hotwife Story

Lacey Cross

CHAPTER 1

I'm stretched out in a lounge chair by the pool, soaking up the sun, and feeling a mix of regret and lust. Regret because I've wasted my chance to sleep with another guy while my husband Greg is away for eight weeks. And lust? Well, that's because I haven't had anything inside me other than toys for those eight weeks. It doesn't help that my favorite toy broke soon after Greg left, and I've been making do with my second favorite one... but it's just not the same. Why didn't I replace that dang thing as soon as it broke?

Let me back up a bit. I'm Sarah, and I just turned 35. I'm married to a wonderful man named Greg, and things have grown a little stale in the bedroom. I guess that's the best way to put it. We got married eight years ago, and that seven-year itch is no joke. For a while now, all I've been able to think about is how I'm never going to experience wild sex. Greg, bless his dear, wonderful soul, is a lover through and through. He knows I wish he could be a little more rough with me, but it's just not in his nature.

My life just feels so damn boring. We live in Greg's childhood home, surrounded by people he's known forever. I can see my future stretching out before me, a monotonous blur that's slowly draining my spirit. Greg keeps encouraging me to get out and meet people or try new things. I should take those painting classes I'm always talking about…I'll wait until fall though, it's too nice lounging around the pool all summer.

In the midst of this stagnation, Greg's career as a hotel general manager has taken an interesting turn. This summer, he's been away opening a new property in another state. Before leaving, he surprised me with what he called a "hotwife-for-the-summer pass"—permission to choose one guy to have fun with during his absence. The only condition? I'd have to share all the details with him later. It was a shocking proposition that stood in stark contrast to our otherwise predictable life.

I thought I'd take him up on it, honestly. I mean, a girl's got needs, right? But here I am, one day before Greg's due back, and I've barely gone anywhere to find another guy. It's been hot this summer, and my motivation to do anything is low. Did I think a guy was going to just drop into my lap? Yeah, I should be so lucky. The universe really should have provided someone for me to fuck, without me having to work for it.

Meanwhile, our neighbors, Jenny and Steve Anderson—a lovely couple in their 50s that Greg has known his entire life—are spending the summer touring Europe. They asked me to maintain their pool while they're away, offering me the chance to use it in return. I was more than happy to agree—it's a damn nice pool, and it's been a lifesaver during the hot summer months.

It's their pool I'm sprawled out beside, in a skimpy white bikini. I've got a nice body—I work hard for it, with yoga and Pilates and running. My red hair is pulled up in a messy bun, and I've got sunglasses perched on my nose. I look like a pinup model: hourglass figure and long, tanned legs. Too bad Greg isn't here to appreciate it.

But inside, I'm a mess. I'm torn between needing to fuck someone—anyone, really—and feeling guilty about it. I love Greg. I really do. But the thought of having one wild, no-strings-attached night with a stranger is…well, it's hot. It doesn't help that this hotwife-for-the-summer pass was his idea. I have a hard time believing he wants me to fuck someone else, but he seems to, if the number of times he's asked me over text if I've found someone yet is any indication. I'm probably going to regret this missed chance for the rest of my life.

Deep in thought, I'm startled by the sudden sound of the sliding glass door opening behind me. My head whips around in shock. Someone's here?

An unfamiliar man with a glass of water in his hand steps out of Jenny and Steve's house. He's a tall, imposing figure with dark hair and a scruffy beard that gives him a rugged appeal. He's wearing a pair of faded jeans and a tight black t-shirt that does little to conceal his muscular physique, particularly his well-defined arms. My eyes are drawn to the intricate tattoos snaking up his forearms... oh yeah, this guy is hella sexy.

I sit up, feeling a jolt of excitement. Who the hell is this guy? And why is he coming out of the Andersons' house? He looks too much at home with his glass of water to be a burglar. They didn't tell me anyone else would be using the house while they were gone. I've been coming and going as I pleased, often in nothing but a bikini. How long has he been here? Has he been watching me? The thought of this hot stranger seeing me half-naked makes my heart race.

He approaches the pool, his eyes fixed on me. I feel a rush of heat between my legs as I take in his intense, passionate stare. He's definitely checking me out—and I'm definitely enjoying it.

He stops a few feet away from me. "Hi there," he says, his voice deep and rough. "I'm Cole. I'm Jenny's brother."

Oh man, that voice does things to me deep inside, and I blink to clear the immediate fog of lust. Jenny never mentioned she had a brother. And even if she did, why the hell didn't she tell me he'd be staying here?

"Sarah," I say, holding out my hand. "I'm the neighbor. I'm taking care of the pool while Steve and Jenny are away."

He takes my hand, his grip strong and firm. I feel a zing of electricity pass between us as our skin touches. It's been eight long weeks since I've felt a man's touch that I'm almost dizzy from it.

"Nice to meet you," Cole says with a hint of a smile. "Mind if I join you?"

I hesitate for a moment, wondering if this is a good idea. But then I remind myself that I'm a grown-ass woman, and I can make my own decisions. And besides, it's not like I'm going to jump his bones right here by the pool... though someone should tell my pussy that.

"Sure," I say, gesturing to the lounge chair next to me. "Have a seat."

Cole has the vibe of a man who knows how to satisfy a woman, and I'm reacting to it. What would he do if I suggested he bend me over the patio table and fuck me right now?

He sits down, stretching out his long legs, and setting his drink next to mine on the small table between us. I try not to stare at the bulge in his jeans, but it's hard—pun intended. I wonder what he's packing under there?

We make small talk for a while, chatting about the weather and the neighborhood. He tells me he's just passing through town, and he needed a place to crash for a few nights. Jenny offered him the house, and he jumped at the chance.

I can't help but feel a pang of disappointment when he tells me he's leaving soon. Not that it matters; Greg is coming home tomorrow. But this is exactly the kind of guy I would fuck if I had more time to get to know him.

I push the temptation aside, reminding myself that I don't need another man—a stranger, for that matter—to sexually satisfy me. I have Greg, and he's great in bed and makes sure I always find pleasure... but he's missing this dangerous, sexy vibe that Cole has. A vibe that says he'll fuck a girl, take what he wants, and leave her a wet mess on the floor when he's done. What would that be like?

My mouth goes dry at the thought. I need a drink. When Cole and I reach for our waters at the same time, our hands brush against each other. A tingle of awareness runs through me. Oh yeah, this guy is dangerous. He could have me on my knees with his cock in my mouth before I could even say "yes, please."

We finish our drinks and make our goodbyes, and I head back to my house, feeling more aroused than I've been in days. I take a long, cool shower, trying to wash away the dirty thoughts that are swirling in my head. But no matter how hard I try, I can't shake the image of Cole's smoldering eyes, his strong hands, that muscular body. Greg needs to be home right now, dammit.

I lay in bed that night, tossing and turning, unable to sleep. I reach for my vibrator, but even that doesn't do the trick. Fucking second best vibrator. I'm ordering myself a new one in the morning. But even if I had my favorite toy, I don't think it would be enough. I need more—I need a man's touch, a man's body.

And that's when I make a decision.

I'm going to fuck Cole.

Right after I make sure it's still okay with Greg.

CHAPTER 2

The next morning, I wake up with a sense of purpose and that lingering question. I need to know if Greg is still on board with this wild idea. I slip into my sexy black lingerie set that is Greg's favorite, and silky robe, letting it hang open just enough to tease. I take a selfie before dialing Greg's number.

"Good morning, beautiful." Greg's voice is thick with sleep, but there's an undercurrent of excitement, as if he's happy to hear my voice. I love how he never gets cranky if I call him and wake him up. I really found myself a keeper, and hopefully he'll still want me to fuck another guy.

"Morning," I purr, running a hand along my thigh. "I've got something to tell you."

I can almost hear him smiling over the phone. "Oh? Do tell."

"Well," I begin, biting my lip. "I met someone. He's...he's really something, Greg."

There's a pause, and then he chuckles. "Is that so? And what did this 'something' say when you told him about our little arrangement?"

Oooh, I think Greg's still on board with me fucking someone. "I haven't told him yet. But I'm planning to. Today."

Greg groans, "Fuck, that's hot. Are you trying to kill me?"

"Mmm, wait a second, I've got a picture for you." I quickly send him the lingerie selfie.

I hear his sharp intake of breath as he opens it. "So sexy, you know I love that bra on you."

Oh yeah, it drives him crazy. "Babe, I need to know you're still okay with this."

"Sarah." His voice is husky. "You know I am. Just promise me you'll tell me everything when I get home tonight."

"I promise," I say, feeling a tingle of lust. Our conversation continues and I tell him about meeting Cole, and how he's staying at the Andersons' house. The longer we talk and tease each other, the more worked up we get. By the time we say goodbye, I'm convinced that this is what we both want.

With determination, I pick my outfit; a revealing sundress that accentuates my cleavage. It ends right above my knees, and I pair it with high heels so my legs look long and sculpted. I sweep my hair up into a ponytail and apply makeup, making sure I look hot as hell. My goal is clear: I want Cole to be unable to resist me.

Clutching my purse, I make my way to the Andersons' house. As I approach, my heart races at the sight of an unfamiliar truck in the driveway. Assuming it belongs to Cole, I feel a surge of excitement. Good, he's here.

I stand nervously in front of the door, my heart beating fast, as I knock. The sound seems to reverberate through the silence, amplifying my self-consciousness. I really hope he doesn't laugh in my face when I try to seduce him.

After what feels like forever and a day, Cole opens the door and stands in the entryway. He's wearing only gray sweatpants, and his bare chest looks yummy. I imagine reaching out and touching him. I've got it bad for this guy.

"Sarah," he says with a smile, and his eyes down the length of me. "Can I help you with something?"

Oh shit. My mind goes blank. I hadn't thought of what to say when I got here. I feel my face getting hot as I struggle to speak.

As Cole's eyebrow rises, I blurt out, "I came to see you—to ask you to fuck me."

He stares at me, not saying anything. The longer the silence lasts, the more I want to run away and forget this ever happened. Why did I say that? He must think I'm crazy. Who just says something like that?

Suddenly, something changes in his expression. His eyes darken, and I can see the desire in them. My body responds, my nipples hardening, and I can feel the tension between us.

He steps back, letting me in. Once the door is closed, he turns to me with a look that says he wants to eat me up...and I'm ready for it.

His voice is firm when he asks, "Does your husband know you're here?"

The gravelly tone of his voice turns me on even more, and I can feel the slickness between my thighs. "Yes, he knows. I have his permission."

He tips his head as if he's thinking, his eyes narrowing slightly. "Show me proof. I don't fuck cheaters."

What the hell? My face burns and I'm not sure if it's from embarrassment or lust. I'm caught off guard by his blunt demand. This guy is making it way too hard to get into his pants...those delicious gray sweatpants that cling to his hips, tempting me to just reach out and push them down to get to what I really want.

I bite my lip, torn between frustration and growing arousal. When I don't respond immediately, he adds, "If you can prove it, I'll make sure you go home to your husband with so many orgasms, you won't remember your own name."

A shiver races down my spine as my eyes widen in response. The air between us is charged with unspoken anticipation, making any coherent thoughts nearly impossible. Within seconds, I'm fumbling with my purse, my fingers trembling slightly as I dig out my phone and text my husband.

Babe, just double checking that it's okay if I fuck Cole.

As I press send, my stomach twists with anxiety. I silently pray to any god who might be listening that Greg is paying attention to his phone. The wait feels like an eternity, and I can feel Cole's eyes on me, watching my every move.

When I see the chat bubbles pop up, I sigh in relief, my shoulders relaxing. My eyes scan the screen eagerly:

Yes, now go over there and get that pussy stuffed so I have something to look forward to tonight.

My husband's crass words make my stomach flutter with happiness. A grin spreads across my face as I look up at the neighbor, newfound confidence surging through me. Fuck, I love Greg for this.

I turn the phone screen towards Cole, my voice husky with desire as I say, "There's your proof. Now, are you going to make good on that promise?"

Instead of answering, he takes the phone from me. I squeak when he starts typing something to my husband. Who does this? His cock better be worth it.

He hands the phone back to me and shows me the message he sent.

This is Cole, the neighbor guy. I'll send her home well used and full of cum.

My mouth forms an 'O' as my husband's reply pops up.

Thanks. Enjoy.

He ends the message with a smiling emoji. I almost laugh, but Cole distracts me by taking my phone and purse, and setting them on a side table next to the couch.

"Now, Sarah, let's talk about this."

Crossing my arms stubbornly, I push my chest out and give him my sassiest look. "Or we skip the talk and you just fuck me."

He smirks, a wicked glint in his eyes, and sits down on the couch. When he leans back, casually draping one arm along the back, he exudes an air of confidence that makes me want to beg him to fuck me. With his free hand, he pulls his gorgeous cock out of his sweatpants and starts stroking it, his movements slow and deliberate.

"Is this what you want?"

My eyes follow his hand, mesmerized. His cock is thick—thicker than anything I've ever had inside me, with a slight upwards curve. My mouth waters just looking at it. Shit, he probably knows he's got an impressive piece of man-flesh right there.

When I realize he's waiting for an answer, I focus on his face and try to use my sexiest voice. It comes out breathier than I intend. "Yes, I want your cock."

He continues to stroke himself as he speaks, his gaze locked onto mine, as my insides quiver. "Is it bigger than your husband's?"

His unexpected question shatters the spell he's woven around me, leaving me momentarily stunned. My mind whirls, struggling to formulate a response that won't jeopardize my chances with him.

He must be able to read the confusion on my face because his eyes glint with mischief as he proposes. "Should I send your husband a picture of it and ask him?"

Wow, Cole is sort of a prick... but his arrogance is only heightening my arousal. My pussy clenches, and I can feel myself growing wet, the dampness soaking into my panties. Yep, I like it. He's the type who's going to fuck me hard just to prove he's a god in the bedroom, and I'm getting more desperate for it by the minute.

When he makes a move like he's going to reach over for my purse, a flurry of panic makes me blurt out, "It's bigger!"

With a satisfied smile he settles back down, continuing to stroke himself with slow, tantalizing motions. "Now was that so hard?"

I want to grumble that Jenny's got an asshole for a brother, but I don't want to ruin my chances of getting that magnificent cock inside me.

"So here's how it's going to go…"

His voice, deep and commanding, draws my attention up from his mouth watering hardness and I fight to focus. I swear I do. But the hypnotic motion of his hand, gliding effortlessly along his length, keeps making me look down. It's driving me crazy.

He speaks with an unnerving calmness that sends a thrill through my core, like he knows I'm going to do exactly what he wants. "You're going to suck my cock. Then, if you ask nicely enough, I'm going to fuck you."

I open my mouth to protest, but he continues. "Now, I'm a nice guy, so I'm going to check in occasionally." His eyes flicker down to my lips before returning to mine, intense and unyielding. "If you ever don't like something, just say 'red light' and I'll stop. Green means everything is good. Understand?"

The room seems to shrink around me, the air thickening with desire. A whirlwind of mixed emotions churns within me, but mostly it's excitement, and a desperate hunger for what he's offering. Is he going to be rough enough that I'll need to use the safeword? Oh god, I've always wanted to be spanked. The thought of him spanking me hard sends a bolt of longing straight to my clit.

I nod and whisper, "Yes. Red to stop, green to continue."

I need this fucking orgasm. He better give me the earth-shattering pleasure he promised. I know he can deliver—hell, his voice alone will probably make me come. The way he's talking to me is hitting some part of me that I didn't even know existed. I love how he doesn't seem to care what I want.

"Good," he growls, his voice dropping an octave as he spreads his knees apart. "Now crawl over here and suck my cock like a good girl."

The command in his voice triggers a primal reaction within me, the urge to submit to his every demand. The phrase 'good girl' has an intoxicating effect on me, and I'm ashamed at how much it makes me want to please him, even while I have to bite back a moan of ecstasy. I didn't know how much I craved this, how easily this man could unravel me so completely.

Without conscious thought, I step out of my high heels and sink to the floor. The dark look in his eyes is intoxicating and I can't look away as I crawl between his knees. This is nothing like what I thought would happen when I came over here, but the unexpected is what makes it so erotic. I can't believe I'm willingly following his orders, but I don't want to stop.

I gaze up at him, suddenly unsure. I swallow nervously. "Can I touch it?"

I just want to feel that girthy cock in my mouth and hands, that's all.

He shakes his head. "No. Put your hands behind your back."

His command is like a spark, igniting a fire within me. I'm tempted to pout, to argue, but instead, I clasp my hands behind my back as instructed. He leans down and wraps my hair around his hand, using it to lift my mouth to his cock. His scent, musky and masculine, fills my nostrils, making my head spin with desire.

"Open," he commands and presses my face closer to his crotch.

I obey, opening my mouth as wide as I can, and he slowly pushes his cock inside, filling my mouth completely. The salty taste of his precum makes me moan, the sound muffled by his shaft. I close my lips around him, sucking hungrily, and I tremble with need.

His grip on my hair tightens, sending a rush of pleasurable-pain through me as he growls, "Good girl."

Fuck, why do I love it so much when he calls me that? This is messed up, twisted, but I just want to do whatever he commands so he'll say it again.

He pushes me down, forcing his cock into the back of my throat, making me gag. "Don't forget to breathe. Relax," he says, his voice soothing yet commanding.

I can feel my throat constricting around him, and I try to listen to his words so I don't choke. Tears sting my eyes, blurring my vision as my body quivers with the effort.

"I know you're enjoying this. I can practically smell how wet this is making you. You love to be treated like a fucktoy."

Shit, he's right. My inner thighs are a mess and the more he treats me like I don't matter, the more I crave it. How did he know something that even I didn't know?

He pulls me up so I can take a deep breath. My pussy is tingling, and I can't deny that this is the hottest sexual experience of my life—and all he's done is shove his cock in my mouth. He pushes me back down onto his shaft, fucking my face. Each thrust makes me crave more.

"Is this what you wanted when you came over here—to be treated like a hole for me to use?"

He pulls my head up again, long enough for me to answer, "I don't know," before he pushes me back down on his cock.

And I really don't know. Is this what I wanted? I've been wishing for a different experience–something that Greg wasn't giving me. A small part of me thinks this is it. Greg loves me so much and worships the ground I walk on. He'd never be able to treat me like this.

I'm lost in my thoughts, so it surprises me when he tugs on my hair, pulling his cock out of my mouth with a wet pop. I sit back on my heels, watching as he stands up, his cock glistening with my saliva.

"Follow me," he says, his voice heavy with desire.

Unclasping my hands from behind my back, I make a move to stand, but he stops me. "No. Crawl."

Oh god. Is he really going to make me crawl to the bedroom? I blush all over at the thought, but I obey like a good girl. He leads me down the hallway, the carpet soft under my knees, and I'm glad the Andersons don't have hardwood floors. I can feel my wet thighs brush together with every step. He brings me into a bedroom, and I stop and kneel in the middle of what is obviously Jenny and Steven's room. I probably should be disgusted by the thought of fucking on their bed, but the naughty buzz from my pussy tells me I'm not. Well, this makes everything more messed up.

A king-sized bed dominates the room, flanked by a dresser and a vanity with a padded chair. A woman's silk robe lies carelessly discarded over the chair. Cole reaches for the sash, the soft fabric slipping through the loops, before he moves behind me.

"I'm going to tie your wrists together," he announces.

It's an unspoken agreement, an invitation to surrender control. The rational part of me knows he's giving me a chance to tell him not to, but fuck if I'm doing that. Not when everything inside me craves the thrill of submission.

With my eyes closed, I feel my heart pounding as the sash gently binds my arms behind my back. Every sensation becomes heightened–the soft brush of fabric against my skin, the growing tightness in my muscles as I test the restraints. The realization hits me: I'm willingly submitting to a stranger, allowing him to tie me up and have his way with me. Despite the unfamiliarity, or perhaps because of it, an intense heat of arousal courses through me. This is so amazingly erotic.

Once he ties me up, he pauses. I turn my head to look at him, puzzled, until I see his predatory expression. His voice drops to a low rumble, sending a thrill of excitement through me.

"Up on the bed. Ass in the air."

I get to my feet, struggling without the use of my arms and somehow manage to climb onto the bed. I take a moment to wonder how I'm going to put my ass in the air, but he helps me by shoving my shoulders down until I faceplant on the mattress. I turn my face so my cheek is pressed against the comforter as I feel him pull my dress up to my waist. This is a strange experience and if anyone had questioned me about crawling for some guy and being bound with my hands behind my back in this position, I would have said 'no thanks.' But this guy has me so needy and desperate that I'd almost do anything he asks. I want him to use me however he wants.

He whistles softly in appreciation as he pulls my panties down to my knees and runs his hand over the curve of my ass. "Such a good slut. So obedient."

I playfully wiggle my hips, eliciting a soft chuckle from him. "Greedy too."

A sharp slap lands on my ass and I cry out in surprise. My face flushes as wetness floods my pussy.

"Color?" he asks.

I fucking love this and moan, "Green."

The next slap hits the other cheek, and I writhe in pain and rapture. How does he know exactly what I want?

"Good girl," he murmurs. "Take it like a good slut."

I'm ready for more, and my pussy throbs with delight. "Green! More."

"You're a kinky little minx." He laughs as his fingers dip between my legs to swirl over my clit.

Fuuuck. Electricity zings from my clit and I buck my hips, trying to get him to rub faster. It seems like what he's doing shouldn't be turning me on this much, but I can't control my response. Everything feels fabulous.

He slips a finger inside me, pumping in and out before adding another one. I moan as he finger fucks me and finds the perfect spot to massage while he brings his other hand between my legs to rub my clit. His fingers are thick, and the combination of pleasure is overwhelming.

I can feel a familiar wave building inside me, and I cry out, "Yes, I'm going to come!"

Instead of encouraging me, he removes his fingers.

"Why?" I wail, frustrated.

He slaps my ass. "Because you didn't ask nicely."

Ugh, damn him. I shamelessly roll my hips and beg, "Please. Please let me come."

"That's better," he says, his fingers resuming their blissful assault on my clit and pussy.

It's as if the denied orgasm multiplies the delight, and the pressure builds more intensely. I cry out in ecstasy as the dam bursts, my orgasm sweeping over me, shaking me to my core. "Ahh, fuck yes," I groan.

Cole hums approvingly, his fingers continuing to drive into me, and I quiver as aftershocks of joy radiate through me.

"Fuck me, please," I whimper, needing to feel his length inside me.

He stops playing with my pussy so he can grab onto my thighs and pull me closer to the edge of the bed until my feet are hanging off. My wrists are still bound, and my face is still smashed into the bedding. This position should be awkward, but I'm beyond caring.

I feel the tip of his cock at my entrance before he slides it up and down my slit. When he teases my clit with the head of his cock, I press my ass back towards him in an attempt to get him to slide in. "Please?"

"I love to hear you beg," he says with a rough groan.

His fingers digging into my hips is the only warning right before he slams his cock into me. Pleasure pulses deep in my core as he bottoms out and pauses. I can already tell that my next orgasm is going to be mind-blowing.

The thought is cut off as he jackhammers into me. Every nerve in my body lights up from delight. Holy fuck. This is exactly what I need.

Cole keeps one hand on my hips as I moan incoherently into the blanket.

"Yeah? You like it hard? You want more?" He starts thrusting harder and deeper, ramming me into the mattress.

I moan in rapture and relief as he tugs at my hands, bringing me upright. "Say you're just a dirty little fucktoy who wants to be used," he demands.

The words tumble out of my mouth, "I'm a dirty fucktoy. Use me!" The ecstasy is so intense I barely hear myself when I start to chant, "Fuck me, fuck me, fuck me," as I writhe in his grasp, impaled on his cock.

He pumps into me, and the force of his thrusts combined with the delicious lack of control over what he's doing to me sends me into a frenzy. I'm moaning and crying out with each thrust, and I can't last long with this constant barrage against my sweet spot.

The euphoria is so intense, I cry out, "Oh god, I'm going to come."

"Come for me you little whore."

He doesn't slow down as he pounds into me, and his dirty words push me over the edge. My body goes rigid as I explode. Wave after wave of pleasure radiates through me, and his thrusts slow while my pussy pulses around his cock.

"That's it, come all over my cock. Show me how much you love it."

Holy fuck. I didn't even know I could feel this much joy. It's as if I'm floating somewhere outside of my body and it takes me a moment to come down and feel grounded.

He lets me rest briefly before pulling out and untying my wrists. When he flips me over onto my back, the fierceness of his expression tells me he's not done using me.

He moves me up into the center of the bed before peeling my panties all the way off. He settles between my legs and immediately drives into me, resuming his brutal pace. I gasp and moan as the oversensitive nerves fire up again. Oh, holy fuck!

I wrap my legs around his waist and my arms around his shoulders. I can tell he's holding back as I scratch and claw at him in a frantic attempt to find purchase as his body slides against mine with each pounding thrust. His cock fills me completely, stretching my pussy and nudging me to another orgasm.

"Oooh, fuck. I'm coming!" I cry out as bliss skyrockets me into another plane of existence.

The ecstasy is unlike anything I've experienced in the past. It sears my brain, consuming me and taking over my entire being. I cling to him as my mind fogs, and my eyes drift closed as I focus on the final tremors. There's an explosion of color behind my eyelids as he continues to fuck me, seeking his own release.

Time suddenly has no meaning, and I'm in a haze of euphoria. I come again and suddenly it's like a never-ending orgasm. I can hear him say something about being his little fucktoy but I'm so far gone, I don't fully comprehend his words.

He pins my wrists to the bed and I lie there as he slams into me. When he finally erupts, he groans and I feel the warm spurt of his cum deep inside me. He shudders and whacks against me a couple more times before he releases my wrists and rolls off me. I feel sweaty, exhausted, and euphoric all at once.

I sigh happily, and mentally drift for a few minutes, enjoying the pleasurable aftershocks running up and down my body. Eventually I crack my eyes open to look at him, but he's just lying on his back, his eyes closed.

When he senses my gaze, he turns to me with a grin. "Well, that was unexpected."

I blink a few times to clear the haze. His entire demeanor has changed, and the cold jerk has been replaced with a relaxed and happy man. That's the power of the pussy right there.

Cole rolls onto his side to face me, and he takes my hand, squeezing it before raising it to his lips to press a kiss to my palm. "So, did I live up to the fantasy of fucking the neighbor while your husband was away?"

I'm not sure how to respond and I can feel myself blushing. I end up smiling and mumbling, "Mmm hmm."

He laughs and climbs off the bed. "I'll be right back, you need water."

I watch him leave, confused about how I'm feeling. There's a lot of thoughts swirling in my head, and I haven't quite come down from the endorphin rush. Now that the moment's over, I'm wondering if Greg would approve if he knew everything I just did. Maybe Cole was too much? What am I going to tell Greg when he asks me how it went?

"Here, drink." Cole interrupts my thoughts as he returns with a glass of cold water. I sit up and drink it, enjoying the way it soothes my dry throat. He gets onto the bed next to me and gently strokes my arm.

"Hey, you okay? Do you need anything?"

"Yeah, I'm fine," I say with a shaky smile. "I was just thinking about how this would affect my marriage. That's all."

Cole squeezes my arm reassuringly. "Your marriage is strong. Trust me, it'll be fine. It'll be the hottest story you two can share."

I look up at Cole and nod. I don't know if he's right about that, but I hope so. "Did I do okay? Did you like it?"

He brushes a lock of hair behind my ear before leaning down to kiss me. "You were phenomenal, Sarah. Truly."

His words make me smile. "Thank you."

After I drink at least half the water, he helps me out of bed and holds me steady as he helps me put my panties back on. I giggle at how my legs feel like Jell-O. When he walks me to the door, I collect my purse and pick up my shoes. No way am I going to teeter home in them with how I'm feeling.

He pulls me in for a soft kiss right before I leave. "Are you going to be okay?"

"Oh yeah, I'm going to take a shower and wait for my husband."

He flashes a grin. "Glad to be of service."

I smile shyly and say, "Thanks again. I had a really great time."

Cole holds open the door for me, and watches me as I head to my house. When I'm halfway across the lawn, he calls out, "Hey, Sarah?"

I pause, turning back.

"Tell Greg that the next time he calls me and asks me to fuck you, we should do it when he's home so he can watch. It would be nice to catch up with him after all these years."

My mouth drops open as he closes the door with a laugh.

Oh. My. God. Greg arranged this! I can't wait until my husband gets home.

CHAPTER 3

As soon as my husband walks through the door, I'm all over him. My desire for him is unbearable after this morning. I'm burning up with lust for my husband, and I need his cock.

He barely has time to laugh out a, "Hello," and drop his bag before I'm yanking all his clothes off. I showered earlier and spent the rest of the day in a robe, so I'm naked within seconds. Our clothes are scattered everywhere as we stumble into the bedroom, not stopping until we hit the bed.

I push Greg down on his back and straddle his lap, kissing him like my life depends on it.

"Fuck, I should have called Cole months ago," Greg moans between kisses.

"Shut up and give me that cock."

I reach between us and line him up with my pussy before sinking down on him. His eyes glaze over with lust, and I know that I've pushed him past the point of no return. He pulls me down, crushing his mouth to mine as his cock presses up into me.

"Tell me about Cole," he murmurs. "Is his cock as big as he always bragged about?"

I take a few moments to appreciate how wonderful it is to be filled by the man I love as I contemplate where to begin. Should I explain how hard I came, or just ride him within an inch of his life? Nah, he's asking....

I begin to grind on his cock and say, "Oh, he's huge."

Greg moans and his eyes roll back in pleasure as I start telling him exactly what Cole did to me. It's not long before he flips us over so I'm under him, our movements urgent as we chase our release.

"Did you love it?" he gasps between deep thrusts.

The ecstasy builds until I can't contain it anymore, and I cry out, "Yes!" as my climax rips through me like wildfire. I shudder from the intensity of it and it triggers Greg's orgasm. When he blows his load I can tell it's a good one from the way his body quakes. He fills me with more cum than he has in ages, and when he's done, he flops down onto the bed next to me, out of breath.

I can feel the wetness leaking out of me and I smile. That's two loads of cum today. I snuggle against my husband, content and fulfilled in a way I haven't felt in a very long time.

He rubs my back and asks softly, "Did he give you exactly what you needed?"

I tip my face to his, grinning. "Oh, yes. Your *old friend* seemed to know exactly what I wanted. Imagine that."

His lips quirk in response. "Always nice to have a buddy you can call on when you need help."

My smile stretches wider and I lick my lips, making sure my husband sees it before I ask, "So...what would you say if I told you Cole suggested that next time you should watch while he fucks me?"

Greg laughs and his, "We'll see," fills me with warmth.

We'll see, indeed.

The End

HOTWIFE FOR THE FALL

A MFM First Time Hotwife Adventure

Lacey Cross

Chapter 1

I'm at my desk, grading papers, when a soft knock at the classroom door interrupts my focus. I glance up and—holy shit—there's a goddamn Adonis standing in my doorway. Tall and broad-shouldered, with dark, tousled hair that screams rugged rather than sloppy. His twinkling grey eyes are framed by laugh lines, adding a touch of maturity to his devastating good looks.

He's wearing a simple white t-shirt and jeans, but there's nothing simple about how they cling to his body. I can't help but notice the outline of his muscles, and a tantalizing hint of a tattoo peeking out from under his sleeve. This man is sex on a stick, and I'm suddenly very, very thirsty.

In my single days, I'd have been all over a guy like this. I'm grateful my husband is fine with me appreciating eye candy, but I should probably tone it down at work. Still, there's no harm in enjoying the view, right?

"Hi," he says, his voice a low rumble that I feel deep in my belly. "I'm here to pick up my son, Jamie. I'm his dad, Luke. I thought it was time to meet the teacher properly."

Luke. Luke Summers. The name clicks into place. This is the guy my husband, Alex, went to college with. The one who recently got divorced and moved here with his kid. Alex has told me stories about their wild days, but he never mentioned that his friend was this fucking hot.

I stand up, trying to keep my cool, but I can feel my heart pounding. "Nice to meet you. I'm Rachel, Jamie's teacher—and Alex's wife." I extend my hand, and when he takes it, I swear I feel a spark. His skin is warm, and his grip is strong. Suddenly, all I can think about is what those hands would feel like on other parts of my body.

He smiles at me, and I try to hide my reaction to him. I can't be drooling over my husband's old college buddy and the father of a kid in my class.

"Thanks for taking care of Jamie," he says. "He's had a bit of a tough time with the move, but he seems to be settling in well."

"He's a great kid," I manage to say, my mouth dry. "We're glad to have him here."

Luke lingers for a moment, his eyes locked onto mine, and I feel my breath hitch. Then he nods and turns to leave, and I'm left feeling like my day has been turned upside down. Jesus, that guy is dangerously handsome.

I have a few more hours of work, but I'm distracted the entire time as I daydream about fucking Luke. Thank god my husband encourages me to fantasize about other guys since he enjoys the result. By the time I get home, I'm so worked up that I practically pounce on Alex as soon as he walks through the door.

"Hey, you," he says, laughing as I pull him close. "What's gotten into you?"

"You better be prepared to fuck me." My hands are already working on his belt.

He raises an eyebrow but doesn't argue, which is one of the many reasons I love him. Within minutes, we're on the couch, clothes discarded, with me straddling him while I bounce on his cock with desperate urgency.

"God," he pants, his hands grasping my hips as I rotate them to wring the most pleasure from his cock deep inside me. "What got you so riled up?"

I grin, my breath coming in gasps as I feel my orgasm building. "I met your friend Luke today," I admit. "He's fucking hot."

Alex's eyes widen, and I feel his cock pulsate inside me. His fingers dig into the flesh of my hips as he forces me to grind against the base of his shaft. "Is that right? Well, I guess I'll have to fill you full of cum and remind your pussy who it belongs to, won't I?"

"Fuck, yes," I pant as his words send me into a frenzy.

Right before I come, Alex flips me onto my back, his powerful arms hooking under my knees, spreading me wide open. He pounds into me, driving his cock deeper and deeper with each thrust. I can feel every inch of him stretching me, filling me. My body is on fire, my nerves tingling with pleasure and excitement.

"You're mine," Alex growls, his eyes locked on to mine. "Say it."

"I'm yours," I gasp, my hands clutching at the couch cushions. "Always."

He gives me that wicked smile of his that always drives me crazy. "Damn right you are."

He leans down, capturing my mouth in a fierce kiss. His tongue invades my mouth, claiming me, possessing me. I kiss him back just as hard. He feels so good, so right. This is what I need, what I always need. Alex.

But even as he fucks me, even as he sends me spiraling into another orgasm, I can't shake the image of Luke from my mind. That rugged face with a body built for sin. I imagine Luke watching us, his eyes filled with lust as Alex fucks me. I imagine Luke joining us, his hands on my body, his cock filling me alongside Alex's.

The thought sends me over the edge, and I scream out my release, my body convulsing around Alex's cock. He groans, his hips moving erratically as he chases his own pleasure. With a final, deep thrust, he comes, filling me with heat.

We collapse onto the couch, a tangle of limbs and heavy breaths. Alex pulls me into his arms, his hands gentle as they stroke my skin. "I love you," he murmurs, his voice soft.

"I love you too," I reply, my heart full. And it's true. I love Alex more than anything. But that doesn't stop the thoughts, the fantasies. It doesn't stop the desire that's burning inside me, the desire for more. For Alex, and for Luke.

It's a good thing my husband gets off on the idea of sharing me. This is going to be something I daydream about every time I run into Luke.

Chapter 2

The next day, I wake up to the smell of fresh coffee and stumble out to the kitchen. Alex likes to do yardwork on Saturday mornings, and he always makes coffee for us first. I open the blinds and pour myself a cup. Alex is out in the yard. He's shirtless, his body glistening with sweat, and I practically hum with pleasure as I appreciate the view. Damn, I married one fine man. But even as I think that, my mind keeps drifting back to Luke. Fuck, he's hot too. Those eyes, that body—it's enough to make any woman weak at the knees. I bet those two were a force to be reckoned with on the hearts of the girls at college.

I'm mid-sip when I see him—Luke—jogging down the street, wearing nothing but a pair of running shorts and a t-shirt that clings to his muscular frame. I nearly spit out my coffee. Holy shit, it's like I manifested him, and he's even hotter than I remembered. I watch as he slows down, spotting Alex in the yard. They exchange greetings, and I can see Luke's smile from here, that damn smile that makes me want to do very, very dirty things.

As they talk, I imagine what it would be like to be sandwiched between them—Alex's familiar touch and Luke's...God, I bet it would be heavenly. My heart races as I picture it, their hands exploring every inch of my body, their cocks hard and ready. I shift uncomfortably, feeling the heat pool between my legs. Fuck, I'm getting so turned on just thinking about it, and all it's going to do is drive me crazy.

The men chat for a few minutes before Luke jogs off and Alex comes inside—smelling of fresh cut grass and all man. I quickly try to compose myself, but he knows me too well. He sees the flush in my cheeks and the lust in my eyes. He glances at the window, notices the open blinds, and a smirk plays on his lips as he teases, "Enjoying the view?"

"Maybe," I admit, setting my coffee down.

He steps closer, his hands sliding around my waist. I can feel his hardness pressing against my stomach, and I let out a soft moan. Now this is more like it.

When Alex lifts me up on the counter, I give a surprised squeak, but I'm not complaining. He doesn't just set me on the counter for no reason, so this is heading in a good direction—one I'm fully on board with.

His fingers trail up my thigh, pushing my nightgown up. "You're so wet," he murmurs, rubbing my pussy through my panties. "Were you thinking about Luke fucking you?"

Mmm, this is so naughty. Alex and I have been discussing trying out the hotwife lifestyle, but it's only been talk. I haven't met any guys that I want to actually fuck until now.

I nod as he pushes my panties aside, his fingers stroking my clit. "Y-yes," I moan as the pleasure swirls in my core.

His eyes darken with lust. "You want to fuck him, don't you? You want to feel his cock inside you while I watch?"

His words send a shiver down my spine, and I feel my orgasm building. "Yes," I admit, flexing my hips and grinding my pussy against his hand. "But I also want to be spit-roasted. I want you both to fuck me, to use me."

He lets out a low growl, his fingers moving faster, pushing me closer to the edge. The tension builds, and I close my eyes, ready to explode. But just as I'm about to come, he stops, pulling his hand away. I whimper in protest, and my eyes fly open. What the hell?

He smiles at me, looking smug. "Not yet, baby. I want you to really think about this. Is this what you want?"

My body aches with need. How can he doubt it with how wet I am? "I want it. I do."

He kisses me deeply, his tongue exploring my mouth. When he pulls back, his eyes are filled with promise. "All right, I'll talk to Luke. See if he's up for it."

Whoa...my mind blanks for a second, and I stare at him. Is this really happening? Am I really about to live out one of my wildest fantasies? I can only nod, my breath coming in quick gasps. Alex smiles, kissing me one last time before stepping back.

"Now I have more yardwork to do," he says, glancing down at my soaked panties. "And my dirty girl probably wants a shower."

I try to be mad about him leaving me hanging, but I'm not. I love this side of him. My body buzzes with unspent desire as he walks away.

Shit, I really hope Luke wants to fuck me.

A few hours after breakfast, I'm bent over the washing machine, loading it with clothes, when I feel Alex's hands on my shoulders. He pins me against the machine, and I know exactly what he wants. I can feel the heat of his body behind me as I spread my legs. I've been wet since this morning, daydreaming about sucking on Luke and Alex's cocks, so I'm more than ready for him. Alex doesn't remove my panties, he just pushes them aside and slides into me. The suddenness of it makes me gasp, the sensation of him filling me sending shockwaves of pleasure through my body.

"God, Alex," I moan, gripping the edge of the washing machine for support.

He pulls out fully and then slams into me as he growls, "Luke is coming over in an hour."

Ooooh, hell yeah!

I close my eyes as Alex thrusts deeper, and I enjoy the building pleasure as he continues. "He's going to fuck you. We're going to give you your fantasy."

My mind spins at his words, my body tensing as my orgasm builds. My husband is so fucking amazing. I cry out and push back against him, imagining how tonight is going to go when I get to fuck two cocks.

The daydream is intense, and I'm quickly losing control. But just as I'm about to come, Alex pulls out, leaving me gasping and desperate. He slaps my ass lightly and says, "Go get ready. I'll finish the laundry."

Fuck...fuck...fuck...I stand up, my legs shaky, and turn to face him. He's so mean, and yet I love it.

He grins at me. "And Rachel," he adds, "Promise me you won't make yourself come. I want you wet and needy."

My mind is fuzzy from pleasure, so I just nod and leave him to the laundry. Once I'm in the shower, the hot water cascades over my body, clearing my mind. But it does nothing to ease the ache between my legs. I wash quickly, my mind racing with thoughts of the guys fucking me. This is all happening so quickly, but I don't care. This is the fantasy I didn't even know I had two days ago. It's wonderful.

Stepping out of the shower, I towel off and stand in front of my mirror, naked and flushed. I scan my reflection, tracing the curves and lines of my body, and I can't help but feel a twinge of uncertainty. I know I look good—I've put in the work, and I'm proud of my body—but there's a vulnerability that comes with being naked in front of someone new.

It's been over ten years since I've slept with anyone other than Alex, and I wonder what Luke will think when he sees me. Will he appreciate the softness of my curves? I don't have the perky body of a twenty-year-old anymore, but at thirty-five, I'm still pretty damn sexy. I take a deep breath, trying to calm my nerves. Luke wouldn't have agreed to come over if he didn't want to fuck me, and that thought gives me the confidence I need. I know I'm ready for this, but that doesn't stop the gentle flutter of butterflies in my stomach. Thank god Alex is going to be with me. I'm not sure I'd want to do this without him.

I hear Alex get into the shower, and it spurs me into action. Shit, I better get ready. I decide on a black lace bra and matching thong, the kind that leaves little to the imagination. I slide the thong up my legs, feeling the lace against my skin, and then fasten the bra. When I look at myself in the mirror, a shimmer of desire runs through me. I look like a woman ready to be fucked. I giggle at myself as my nipples harden. Yeah, I'm definitely ready for some cock.

I slip on a blue sundress, the kind that cinches at the waist and flares out slightly, hiding the lingerie underneath but still giving easy access to wandering hands. Since we are staying home, I leave my feet bare. I style my hair down, with the soft, natural blonde waves around my shoulders, and apply a touch of makeup, just enough to highlight my brown eyes.

As I'm finishing up, Alex comes into the bedroom, a towel wrapped around his waist. He looks at me, his eyes taking in the sundress. "You look like a fucking snack," he says, walking over to me. He leans down, his mouth by my ear. "You're such a slut, aren't you? I bet you're dripping wet already."

I shiver at his words. He knows I enjoy being called a slut. But before I can respond, the doorbell rings, and my heart leaps into my throat.

Alex grins at me, drops the towel, and pulls on a pair of jeans. "Ready, babe?"

I have to clear my throat to say, "Yep," and he winks at me as he leaves the room to answer the door.

My heart pounds with anticipation. I can't believe I'm about to fuck Luke. And the icing on the cake is that Alex is going to be a part of this. God, I hope this goes well.

CHAPTER 3

I make my way downstairs, pausing at the foot of the stairs and taking a deep breath to calm the wild beat of my heart. Their low voices rumble from the foyer, and as I round the corner, I see him—Luke, standing there in all his glory. He's wearing a simple green t-shirt and jeans, his dark hair slightly disheveled, like he's run his fingers through it one too many times. When his grey eyes meet mine, I swear I see a spark of hunger.

"Hey, Luke," I say, my voice breathier than I intend.

His gaze sweeps over me, taking in my flushed cheeks, my sundress, down to the pink polish on my toenails. He smiles—a devastating grin that makes my knees weak. "You look gorgeous."

I feel my cheeks flush a brighter pink at his words. Before I can respond, he steps closer, his hand reaching up to brush a strand of hair behind my shoulder. His touch sends a shiver down my spine, and I fight the urge to sway towards him.

"Alex tells me you have a fantasy," he murmurs, his eyes locked onto mine.

I nod, wishing I could be one of those confident women who asks for exactly what she wants, but Luke is making me tongue-tied.

He leans in, kisses me right below my ear, and whispers, "You want to be a good little slut for us, don't you?"

His words send a jolt of desire through me, and my pussy throbs with need. I nod again and softly moan, "Yes."

He smiles, a slow, predatory grin, as he takes my hand and we follow Alex to the living room. Alex settles on the couch, ready to watch, and I blow him a kiss as Luke positions me in the center of the room. I'm not sure where this is going, but I appreciate that Luke is taking the lead. If it were left up to me, I'd stand around awkwardly until someone just bent me over something and fucked me—not that I'd be complaining.

Luke slides his hands up my arm, igniting a trail of goosebumps that sends a shiver straight to my core. He cups my chin firmly, forcing me to meet his gaze. The hunger in his eyes matches mine and sets my pulse racing. "Get on your knees," he commands, his voice a low growl that pulls at something deep inside me. All I want to do is obey.

I sink to the floor in front of him, and he unbuttons his jeans, slowly pulling out his cock. It's thick and hard, and my mouth waters as I imagine running my tongue along the veins and making him moan. Behind me, the sound of Alex undoing his zipper thrills me. Is Alex going to stroke himself while watching me suck his friend's cock? The thought sends a surge of heat between my thighs.

I don't have a chance to dwell on the thought, because Luke grasps the base of his cock, guiding it to my lips. "Suck," he orders, making my stomach flutter with lust.

My pussy grows wetter as I take him into my mouth, swirling my tongue around the head, tasting the salty pre-cum leaking from the tip. I'm so engrossed in the first new cock I've had in over ten years that I don't realize Alex has gotten off the couch until I feel the head of his cock against my cheek. Oooh, I get to suck on both of them! This is nice and filthy.

I pull off Luke's cock and turn, taking my husband's cock into my mouth. My nipples harden and my body hums with delight as I alternate between the men. My husband's familiar taste and girth make the unknown of Luke even more noticeable. I feel like a goddess, worshipping these two cocks, while their moans fill the room. The longer I suck on them, the fuzzier my mind gets. My mouth is just a hole for their pleasure. They could use me like this all night, and I'd love it.

Without thinking about it, I reach down, slipping a hand between my legs, feeling the wetness there. Luke sees me and tsks, "Not yet, gorgeous. We'll take care of you."

I'm in my happy place, and I don't even mind waiting as I mindlessly suck on each guy. The next time I move to take Luke's in my mouth, Luke stops me and yanks me to my feet. A shiver of anticipation runs through me as he leads me to the couch. He sits down and pulls me into his lap, making me gasp in surprise. My back is to his chest, and he slides his hands under my sundress. His touch is electric, sending waves of heat through me as he explores my thighs, my hips, my stomach. I'm flush with desire, my thoughts a whirlwind of neediness, and all I can think about is getting his cock inside me.

When he cups my breasts, his fingers teasing my nipples through the lace of my bra, I moan and arch into his touch. I grind against him, feeling his cock hard and insistent against my ass, my body eager for more. A sense of urgency washes over me, and I shimmy my hips, hoping the friction will get him to fuck me.

Alex stands in front of us, his cock in his hand, stroking it slowly as he watches. I love that Alex is participating and enjoying this. Luke slips a hand between my legs, pushing my thong aside, his fingers stroking my clit. I moan, my head falling back against his shoulder.

"You like that?" Luke murmurs in my ear. "You like being our little slut, don't you?"

I whimper, "Yes. God, yes."

Luke lifts me slightly, positioning me over his cock. He slides into me, filling me completely. I cry out, my hands gripping his thighs as I ride him. Alex steps closer, pulling off my sundress and dropping it to the floor, leaving me in just my bra and thong. Alex's cock is inches from my face.

No one has to tell me what to do. I take him into my mouth, sucking him in time with my movements on Luke.

The room fills with the wet slap of flesh against flesh, our moans and groans, and the sucking sounds of my mouth on Alex's cock. As I get closer to coming, my movements become more frantic. Luke continues to rub circles around my clit, and I feel my orgasm building.

"That's it, gorgeous," Luke groans. "Come for us. Show us how much you love this."

He presses down firmly on my clit, and I come undone. My body convulses, my screams muffled by Alex's cock. Luke holds me tight as he pistons his hips, fucking me through my orgasm.

As I come down, Alex gently pulls me off of Luke's cock, lifting me into a standing position. My legs are wobbly, my body still tingling with bliss. Before I can catch my breath, Alex bends me over the couch right in front of Luke. I instinctively grab onto the armrest with one hand and place the other on the cushion next to Luke to brace myself. In one fluid motion, Alex slams into my slick, spasming pussy. I cry out in pleasure as he bottoms out. This is intense, and all I want to do is make them come as hard as I just did.

"Fuck, you feel so good," Alex groans as he hammers into me.

Luke's erection juts out in front of my face, glistening with my juices. Without hesitation, I wrap my lips around the tip, sucking hard. The musky taste of our mixed arousals coats my tongue. Luke groans as I sink lower on his shaft, sucking and licking. Alex thrusts so hard, it forces Luke's cock even further down my throat with each whack against my pussy.

The dual sensation of Alex pounding into my pussy from behind and Luke's cock throbbing in my throat is overwhelming. I surrender myself completely to the moment as pleasure ripples from my fingertips to my toes. I'm seconds away from detonating into another explosive climax. Nothing else matters except chasing the white-hot euphoria.

"That's it, gorgeous," Luke growls as his fingers tangle in my hair and he forces himself deeper. I moan around him, sending delicious vibrations up the length of his shaft.

My legs start to wobble, muscles quivering from the impending orgasm. Alex pounds into me harder, and tears spring to my eyes as Luke plunges deep, hitting the back of my throat. Alex is never this rough, and I revel in knowing that I've driven him to this level. Knowing my husband is letting go of his inhibitions makes this experience even more amazing.

Alex gives a long moan, and his pleasure spirals me into my orgasm. As the rapture crashes over me, my pussy clenches around Alex's cock and I cry out around Luke's shaft buried deep in my throat. Wetness gushes out around Alex's shaft, dripping down my thighs, further lubricating his relentless thrusts.

I'm still riding the waves of my orgasm when Alex pulls out suddenly, leaving me feeling empty and desperate for more. Luke's cock pops out of my mouth as I gasp for air, my body trembling with aftershocks.

"Not done with you yet," Luke murmurs, his voice heavy with lust.

Alex helps me stand up, and Luke shares a wicked grin with him as a silent communication passes between them.

"Climb onto Luke's lap, sweetheart," Alex instructs, and I comply without hesitation, my body still humming with need. I straddle Luke, facing him, and position myself over his cock. I sink down on his shaft, moaning, and grip the backrest of the couch. Behind me, I hear the top opening on a bottle of lube and then feel Alex's slick fingers pushing my thong aside and circling my ass. Oh god, yes. I didn't even ask for double penetration, but suddenly it's all I want.

Alex slowly presses a finger into my ass, preparing me. I push back against him, urging him to go deeper. The sensation of Luke's cock in my pussy and Alex's finger in my ass is incredible.

Alex replaces his finger with the head of his cock, slowly pushing into me. I moan loudly, the sensation of being filled by both of them making my head spin. They start to move, finding a rhythm, one thrusting in as the other pulls out. It's intense, overwhelming, and exactly what I need.

"Fuck, you feel so good," Luke groans, his grasp on my hips tightening.

"So fucking tight," Alex grunts as he bottoms out.

I can feel every inch of them, filling me, stretching me, pushing me to the brink. "Fuck, yes," I groan, my hands clutching at the couch as they use both my holes. My body is slick with sweat, my skin hypersensitive as Luke's fingers dig into my hips, his cock driving into me forcefully. Alex's hands are on my ass, spreading me wide, his cock buried deep. I can feel them both, thrusting, grinding, their bodies slapping against mine and hitting all the right spots.

I feel another orgasm building, this one even more intense than the last. My body is on fire, every nerve ending lighting up with pleasure. Luke moves a hand between my legs, his fingers brush against my clit, circling, teasing, sending jolts of pleasure coursing through me. The room is filled with the sound of our moans as our pleasure builds.

My body tenses and I cry out, "Oh god, I'm going to come," as my orgasm rips through me. My vision blurs and my body convulses with wave after wave of pure ecstasy. I can feel my pussy clenching around Luke's cock, my ass tightening around Alex. They both groan, their thrusts becoming more frantic.

"Fuck, Rachel," Luke grunts, his body tensing as he finds his release. His cock pulses inside me as he shoots ropes of sticky cum, filling me up and sending aftershocks of pleasure through my body.

Alex is right behind him, his cock pulsing in my ass. "God, yes," he groans, his body shuddering against mine.

Time holds no meaning, and it feels like they continue to fuck me forever as they fill me with cum. I imagine it dripping out of me for hours, and the thought sends a delicious zip of pleasure through me. This experience is nothing like I expected. It's fucking amazing.

When the guys finally slow down, we collapse in a tangle of limbs. We're slick with sweat, and my heart pounds so loud I swear I can hear it. I can feel them both, still inside me, their cocks slowly softening. I'm spent, my body limp, my mind floating in a haze of pleasure. This is what I wanted, what I craved. And they gave it to me, completely, unapologetically. I smile, my eyes closed, my body pressed between theirs. This is fucking bliss.

I'm not sure how long we stay like this, but eventually they pull out, leaving me feeling empty and satiated all at once. I collapse onto the couch next to Luke, my body still trembling from pleasure.

Alex leaves briefly to clean up and then joins us on the couch. There's a guy on either side of me. I snuggle close to Alex with Luke's warmth against my back, and I sigh in contentment. This is the life.

"So, how was that for a fantasy?" Alex asks as he strokes my back softly.

I laugh. "Better than I imagined."

Luke chuckles, his fingers tracing lazy patterns on my arm. "Glad we could make your dreams come true, gorgeous."

I look up at them, a wide grin on my face. "Thank you. Both of you. That was...incredible."

And it was. It was everything I had hoped for and more. And as I sit there, sandwiched between my husband and his friend, I have the sudden hope that this is just the beginning. Being double stuffed on the regular sounds pretty damn good to me, but even if we don't do this again, I'm going to remember tonight every single time Luke stops by the school.

This is going to be an interesting year, that's for sure.

The End

Hotwife for the Winter

A First-Time Fantasy on Vacation

Lacey Cross

CHAPTER 1

Jack's voice slices through my morning haze. "Holly, I want to discuss my idea."

I glance at him. He's relaxed in his kitchen chair, that familiar spark in his eyes. My heart quickens—I know that look. It's the one that says he's thinking about something naughty...which means I know exactly what he wants to talk about.

I pick up my coffee to buy myself some time. I don't want to act too excited. He's going to have to work for it.

"Oh yeah?" I take a sip and the warm liquid jolts me further awake. "And what about it?"

"I think we should do it. You know, make it happen. It's time we stop just talking and start doing."

Jack gives me a devilish grin, and a shiver of anticipation runs down my spine. He's talking about that crazy idea he's been thinking about for weeks. The one that makes my pulse race.

"Just like that?" I trace the rim of the mug with my finger. "It's not as simple as just deciding to do it. There's a lot to think about."

Jack's eyes smolder. "I know. But I think it's something you want too. You've always had that fantasy, right? About being...used."

A tingling sensation zips straight to my pussy, and I squirm in my seat. Fuck. He knows me too well, but I can't help teasing him. "I don't think you were complaining the night we roleplayed I was a call girl."

Jack laughs. "That was hot." He reaches across the table, taking my hand. His thumb traces circles on my skin, a familiar gesture that always calms me. "You don't have to say yes. But I thought...Vegas. Our trip next month. It could be a good place to start."

Vegas. Damn, that's actually perfect. "And you want to watch me with someone else? Is that the plan?"

"Well, you can't exactly be my call girl since I want you to fuck someone else." He continues his slow circles on my hand, his touch sparking a trail of fire. "I want to see another guy turn you into a little slut. You trust me?"

Pleasure zings through me. He knows exactly what to say to turn me into a wet mess. "Yes."

And I do trust him—completely. That's why this idea is so exhilarating. I wouldn't want to do it without him.

"Then let's do it. And I'll be there, watching every second. Plus, we can try to find a guy who's good at dirty talk, since I'm not."

"I'm in." The words pop out of my mouth before I can change my mind. My nipples tighten as I imagine fucking another guy and being called filthy things while Jack is in the room.

He kisses the back of my hand. "We'll take our time, plan it right."

This is madness. Or is it?

Despite my reservations, I really do want to be a hotwife. If I was going to pick a guy, it would be one who could give me something my husband can't. I don't need to be fucked hard and called a slut to live a happy life, but sometimes–yeah, sometimes I wish I could experience it. I'd never trade my husband for all the dirty talk in the world, but if I'm going to fuck someone else...

I hold in my giggle. Vegas, the city of sin. Seems fitting.

As we launch into plans about how it would work out, and discussions about which holes can be used, I suddenly realize the trip isn't for weeks. My slutty side is ready to embrace being a hotwife. How in the hell am I going to make it a whole month?

CHAPTER 2

The Vegas strip flashes by outside our cab. I bet those lights will dazzle once the sky goes full black. Jack squeezes my thigh and lust simmers in my veins from just that one touch. A month of anticipation has left me buzzing like a live wire. Not just anticipation, though. A month of practicing, too. God, how many times did he bend me over the kitchen counter, the couch, the bed, spinning scenarios about other guys fucking me? We even pretended I was a call girl again. If just the thought of me fucking someone else has revitalized our bedroom time, what will the real thing do for us?

We're dropped off at the grand entrance of a luxury hotel on the strip, and I gawk at the sheer opulence. Jack planned everything, and he chose well. The cold air nips at us as we bustle inside, but the hotel's warmth quickly dispels the February chill.

We make our way through the lobby, and I sense the eyes on me. My blonde hair and generous breasts always draw attention, and usually it makes me self-conscious, but today it's different. Today I love it, and I want to be on display.

Check-in is efficient, and once we're in our room, I let out a sigh. We finally made it.

I check out the room while Jack unpacks a few things. The king-size bed and strip view are stunning, but my mind is elsewhere.

"You good?" Jack wraps his arms around my waist from behind.

I lean into him, enjoying the warmth of his solid chest. "Nervous. Excited. You know how it is."

"Want to hit the pool?" He kisses my neck, and my clit throbs. "It might help you relax before the main event."

The 'event' being us finding someone to fuck me senseless. "Yeah, I think I will. But you won't come because it's too cold."

He laughs. "Yeah, swimming in February is a 'hell no' for me. I'll warm you up when you get back."

He knows how much I enjoy swimming, and the pools are usually the best thing about our trips. His choice of hotel is another reason I love him. During the winter months, he always makes sure to choose places with heated pools that are open year-round.

"Deal." I give him a quick kiss before changing. My bathing suit is a white one-piece with a strategic cutout highlighting my cleavage. It looks as if it was made just for me, and whenever I wear it, I feel sexy and bold. Wrapping a robe around myself, I blow Jack a kiss and swish my ass in his direction as I leave.

The hallway is deserted, and I quickly follow the directional arrows on the walls to the outside recreation area. The air is chilly enough that steam rises from the water's surface. The pool isn't crowded, and there are a few people scattered around enjoying the warm oasis in the cool afternoon.

I slip off my sandals and robe, dropping them onto a lounge chair before diving in. The warm water envelops me, and as I swim a few laps, the stress in my muscles ease. I wish we could afford our own pool, but we're lucky enough that we both have good jobs and can take several mini vacations every year.

My mind races as I relax in the water, and I glance around, taking stock of the other guests. A group of guys catches my attention, all toned and tanned as they joke with each other. Mmm, nice eye candy.

I swim for a bit, trying to distract myself. But I can't stop thinking about having another cock inside me for the first time in 10 years. When I've been swimming long enough that my fingers prune up, I force myself out of the water. I'm shivering as I slip the robe back on. Right before I leave, a guy walks into the pool area and I pause. Oh god, he's gorgeous. He's tall and strong, his muscles defined and taut. His salt-and-pepper hair glistens in the sunlight, which puts him right in my favorite age bracket for fantasy men. Oh yeah, that's one daddy who could dom me anytime he wanted.

I linger a moment, watching him dive in and cut through the water with confidence. I can't see his hands, but I daydream that they're large enough to get a good handful of my breasts as he fucks me from behind. Okay, I should probably stop objectifying every guy I see at the hotel, but fuck, I need a cock in me ASAP.

Giggling at myself, I head back up to the hotel room. When I enter, Jack is on the couch stroking his cock through his jeans and gives me a hungry look. My pussy tingles and I'm ready to pounce on him.

"How was the swim?" He's speaking in a husky tone that always makes me want him.

"Refreshing." I shrug out of the robe and peel my damp suit off, dropping them both on the floor. "But I think I need something more."

He stands up, stalking toward me with a predatory expression. "Is that so?"

"Mmm hmm. I need you to remind me why we're doing this."

"I think I can do that." Jack's lips slant against mine and his tongue sweeps into my mouth. Delight surges through me as I plaster myself against him. Oh yeah, this will do nicely.

The delicious ache from my pussy robs me of all coherent thought. My toes curl the longer the kiss goes on, and I'm beyond caring about tonight. I need my husband right now.

He breaks off the kiss, and I tremble when he moves his mouth to my ear to nibble on the lobe. "You want this, don't you, baby? You want me to watch someone fuck you senseless."

"Yes," I whimper, grinding against him. Fuck yes, I do.

He slides a hand between my legs, and I spread them to give him easier access. He rubs my clit teasingly. "And you're going to come on his cock like a good girl, aren't you?"

Oooh, fuck. Has he been studying up on dirty talk? He's never spoken to me like this before, and I love it. I moan, "Yes, like a good girl."

He slides a finger inside me, fucking me slowly. "And what if I told you I want to see you being used like a little fucktoy? Would that turn you on?"

"Yes, so hot." My head spins as I ride his hand.

He adds another finger. "Good girl. But you're not coming yet."

I whimper as the pleasure increases. "Jack..."

He pulls his fingers away, leaving me throbbing and needy. "Not yet. You can come when another man is fucking you. Now get ready so we can head out."

I blink at him through a fog of lust. Who is this man, and what did he do with my husband?

He smiles like he knows exactly what he's doing to me, and he kisses my nose. "Or we could stay in, and you could be my slutty call girl again tonight."

I get a hold of myself and push at him playfully. "Hey, we're here for me to become a hotwife. We can roleplay at home."

He chuckles, and the sound vibrates through me. "I suppose, but I sort of like the idea of you being a *Vegas* call girl."

Yeah, not happening, buddy. I dance out of his arms and blow him a kiss. "Sorry, someone told me to go get ready. I'm fucking someone else tonight."

I'm giggling as I enter the bathroom and turn on the shower. Under the warm spray, I imagine possible scenarios with other men and I'm tempted to give myself a quick orgasm but resist. The anticipation is all part of the fun. Besides, Jack's out there, rock hard, and he's got a lot longer to wait before he gets relief.

Once the shower is done and I towel off, I find that Jack laid my dress and undergarments out on the bed. As I put on the matching red lace bra and panty set, I wonder who will be taking it off me.

Jack is silent as he watches me dress, and a pleasant longing pulls at me. My dress is a sexy red number that clings to my breasts with a full skirt that ends at the knees. I admire myself in the mirror as I smooth the dress down my thighs. It hugs my curves just right, and the V neckline offers a tantalizing hint of cleavage.

Jack whistles appreciatively. "You look good enough to eat. Bet you're soaked right now."

"Guess you'll find out later." I flash him a coy smile.

He chuckles. "Count on it."

After slipping on a pair of heels and touching up my makeup, Jack offers his arm. "Let's go find someone to make you a hotwife."

My heart flips as arousal zings through me. I'm ready.

CHAPTER 3

The casino pulses with energy—the clink of glasses, the low hum of chatter, and the distant chime of slot machines. Jack guides me through the throng, his hand firmly on the small of my back. I've waited so long for tonight, it's surreal that it's finally here.

We snag seats at a sleek bar, and Jack orders drinks—sparkling water with lime for him, cranberry juice for me. We're staying clear-headed tonight, no booze to blur the lines. I'm tingling with anticipation, and it's difficult to think of anything other than how I'm going to get a cock inside me as quickly as possible. I need to be hunting for a man.

I scan the crowd, and then I see him. The guy from the pool, now dressed in a tailored suit that accentuates his good looks. He oozes confidence and wealth. He's everything I've fantasized about.

Fuck, he's gorgeous. Would I actually have a chance with him?

Our eyes meet, and his seductive smile sends a rush of pleasure through me. Maybe I do.

Jack whispers, "You see something you like?"

I sip my drink, feigning nonchalance. "Maybe. That older guy in the suit—he's hot."

"He is," Jack laughs. "Go get him."

My nerves are a jumble inside me as I rise. Can I even pull this off? It's been ages since I've flirted with anyone but Jack. I bring my drink with me and put a little extra sway in my step, hoping it looks seductive and not ridiculous.

"Is this seat taken?" I ask, gesturing to the empty stool beside him. I'm trying to play it cool despite the flutter in my chest.

He smiles, and it's a good smile—confident, charming. "Not at all. Please, join me."

I sit, and his gaze is like a warm caress. He's definitely checking me out, and it's a rush.

"I'm Holly," I say, extending my hand. My fingers tremble, but I hope he doesn't notice.

He takes it, his grip firm. "Nick. A pleasure to meet you, Holly."

His touch elicits a spark of excitement that makes my stomach flutter. "Likewise, Nick. What brings you to Vegas?"

His eyes roam over me in a way that makes me tingle. "Business. But I'm always open to a bit of fun as well."

Here's my opening. "Is that so? And what kind of fun are you after?"

He gives me a slow smirk. "Well, I think you might already know the answer to that." He pauses before continuing in a lower tone. "But I must admit, I'm curious—do you do this often?"

I blink, caught off guard. "Do what often?"

"If you have terms, we should discuss them now."

Wait—does he think...? Oh god, he thinks I'm an escort. The realization makes my heart race. This is it—this is the fantasy I've played out in my head a thousand times. Pleasure floods through me as the heat builds in my core.

I take a sip of my drink, and my hand shakes slightly as I set the glass down. "And if I do?"

Nick's eyes gleam with desire. "Then I'd say we're in for a very interesting night. So, what are your terms?"

I glance at Jack. I can see the excitement written all over his face even from here. He still looks to be all in on our game.

I give Nick my attention again. "There's something you should know. I'm not...cheap. And there's a condition."

Nick raises an eyebrow. "Oh? And what's that?"

"The guy across the bar..." I nod subtly toward Jack. "He's the one paying. And he wants to watch."

Nick smiles. "I saw you come in with him and assumed he was your husband."

"Would that be a problem for you?" I try to play coy, wanting to keep the fantasy going.

"It doesn't matter one bit to me. I'd fuck you either way." He shifts closer. "So what do you say? Are you up for some fun?"

The thought of being desired and being used for someone's pleasure, thrills me. I can barely keep my composure. "Yes, but I need to talk to him for a moment." I look over at Jack, who gives me a discreet thumbs-up while taking in the scene.

"Of course. I'll be right here."

I stand up and my legs wobble a bit as I make my way back to Jack. Fuck, I hope he's okay with this plan.

When I'm close enough, I rush my words. "So, babe, I sort of let him think I'm an escort. And I told him you're paying for me—and that you want to watch."

Jack's eyes widen for a fraction of a second before he grins. "That's fucking hot. Did you do this for me? You're amazing, you know that?"

Oh thank god. He's okay with it, but I still have to double check. "It was for both of us. But you're good with it? I can tell him we changed our mind, if not."

"Hell yes, I am. Let's do this."

My stomach flutters from excitement as I gesture to Nick to come join us. As he approaches, I admire him again. Damn, I really picked a winner—assuming he's good in bed.

"Nick, this is Jack," I say once he's close enough. "He's the one making this happen."

Nick extends his hand to Jack, and they shake firmly. "A pleasure, Jack. You have excellent taste."

Jack chuckles. "I know I do. And I'm glad you think so too."

"Shall we? I have a suite upstairs." Nick's gaze flicks between us.

Oh god, a suite. This just keeps getting better. "Lead the way."

Nick turns and we follow, the tension palpable. The elevator ride is a blur, and when the doors slide open, we step into a lavish hallway. Nick's room is at the end and the suite is stunning—a sprawling living area with floor-to-ceiling windows overlooking the Vegas strip. But my attention is quickly drawn to the king-size bed in the adjoining room, the plush comforter and pillows looking impossibly inviting.

Nick closes the door behind us. "So, Jack, what exactly are you paying for?"

I hold my breath as I tremble with excitement. Jack's voice is steady. "I'm paying to watch you fuck her and use her. And the more dirty talk, the better."

Yeah, my husband is amazing. He knows I wish he could be more vocal in the bedroom, so his request is sweet and dirty.

Nick's eyes flash with desire. "And if I want to use you like a little plaything? Is that within your terms?"

"Yes, that's exactly what I want."

He gives me a satisfied smile. "Are any holes off limits?"

Jack speaks up quickly. "No anal."

I stand there, my heart pounding, as they negotiate my holes like I'm not even in the room. It's filthy, so filthy, and yet—god, I love it. The bluntness of it, the way they're deciding how I'll be used, makes me tremble with desire.

Nick's smile widens. "Then let's not waste any more time."

Oh yeah, this is going to be good.

Chapter 4

Nick's eyes rake down my body. "Take off the dress."

It's not a request.

My heart beats faster and my fingers tremble as I unzip my dress. The air is cool as the red fabric pools at my feet. I'm left in my red bra and panties, the lace doing little to hide what's underneath.

Nick studies the swell of my breasts and my nipples harden. He nods at my bra. "Now the rest."

I kick my heels off and I unhook my bra, shivering as the lace tickles my arm on its way to the floor. Nick's sharp inhale is a reward, a confirmation that he likes what he sees. My breath hitches as I stand there waiting for his next command.

"Now the panties, and then turn around," he orders.

I obey, and my panties drop to the floor. I face the windows, and the city sprawls below like a glittering audience. He moves behind me and cups my breasts. Mmm, nice. I arch into his touch when he pinches my nipples hard. The mix of pleasure and pain is intoxicating.

"You're here to be used," he growls in my ear. "Not to enjoy yourself."

I moan, knowing that being used is going to be me enjoying it. He grinds his massive cock against my ass. Oooh, nice.

He twirls me around, crushing his lips to mine as his tongue explores my mouth. I claw at his suit jacket, desperate to caress his skin, but he grabs my wrists and holds them together in front of me.

"Patience," he chides, stepping back.

He doesn't strip. "Tell me, how rough do you want it?"

Oh god, he wants me to say it. The illicit thrill of having to admit what I want makes my clit throb. "I want it rough. And...and I want you to call me a slut."

He nods with approval. "Good, but you need a safeword. If it's too much, say 'red.' Understand?"

"Yes." I nod while my pulse quickens. Oh god, is he going to do something that requires a safeword?

When he takes his shirt off, his chest is sculpted, with a faint line of silver hair trailing down his stomach. He unbuckles his belt, the leather whispering through the loops. My mouth waters at the sight of him once he's naked. His cock is thick enough that I'm not sure my fingers could wrap around it, but I'd love to try.

"On your knees, slut," he orders, and I want to obey him immediately.

I sink down, thankful for the soft carpet. He towers over me, gripping his cock—thick, veined, and already glistening at the tip. He taps his cock on my lips, smearing the slick pre-cum across my mouth. "Open up."

I part my lips, and he pushes in, the taste of salt and musk flooding my tongue. He tangles his fingers in my hair, gripping tight enough to send a prickle across my scalp. "Now take it all like a good little slut."

He sinks in slowly, inch by inch, until he hits the back of my throat. I relax my jaw, breathing through my nose as he starts to fuck my face. God, he's huge. Spit runs down my chin and drops onto my breasts as he thrusts deeper. When I gag slightly he eases up, but doesn't stop. He groans loudly, tightening his grip on my hair and tipping my head back to give him better access.

"Look at me," he commands.

I peer up at him. He's watching his cock disappear into my mouth. "Such a pretty little fucktoy. You love being used like this, don't you?"

I moan around his cock, the vibration making him groan. I hope Jack can see all of this. The thought of how dirty this must look to my husband sends a bolt of pleasure straight to my clit. I'm getting wetter, my pussy responding to the sheer filth of it all. The room goes hazy as I focus on the rhythm of his thrusts, the pressure of his fingers in my hair, the way his cock fills my mouth completely.

"Fuck, you're good at this," he pants as he thrusts faster. "You're just a little fucktoy. Just a hole for me to use."

His words send me spiraling. Knowing Jack is here to keep me safe allows me to let go completely. My mind drifts into a warm, fuzzy place and I go limp, surrendering to his control. I'm just a toy, just a thing for him to use. The realization unleashes a twist of dark desire in my brain, and I moan again, the sound muffled by his cock.

He withdraws suddenly, his cock slick and glistening. "On the bed, on your back," he orders. "Spread your legs for me."

I snap back to attention and scramble onto the bed, keeping my feet flat on the mattress while parting my knees. He crawls between my thighs, his gaze fixed on my pussy.

"So fucking wet." He slides two fingers inside me, curling them to massage a wonderful spot.

"Fuck," I gasp when he adds a third finger, stretching me, fucking me with slow strokes.

"You're going to come for me," he commands. "You're going to come all over my fingers and give Jack a show."

Being directed to come for my husband is the right kind of dirty for me. He jackhammers into me faster, and my muscles tense. When he sucks on my clit while finger fucking me, it's too much pleasure. I come hard and convulse around his fingers. He keeps fucking me through it, drawing out every last wave of bliss.

When I finally go limp, he removes his fingers, licking them clean with a satisfied groan. "Such a tasty little fucktoy. But we're not done yet. Get on your hands and knees. I want that ass in the air."

My body responds before my mind can process, and I flip over, presenting myself to him. My arms tremble slightly as I prop myself up. Nick's palm connects with my ass, a crack that echoes through the room. The sting is immediate, a bright flash of heat that blooms into something darker, more urgent. I yelp, but it's not from pain—it's from the sudden, overwhelming need for more.

"Oh, the little slut likes being spanked?" He squeezes the reddened skin. "Do you want more?"

"Yes," I hiss. The sting of his handprint pulses hot and insistent and I cry out, "More!"

He smacks again, harder this time. I jerk forward, and I immediately wiggle my ass, inviting another one. Each spank sends a jolt to my core, the pleasure escalating like a storm.

"Look at you," he murmurs in approval. "Dripping and desperate for it."

His hand lands again, and the pleasurable heat spreads, pushing me closer to the edge.

"Please," I beg, not really sure what I'm begging for. His cock? More? "Don't stop."

He laughs, amused. "Does the fucktoy want to come?"

"Yes," I choke out. I'm trembling and so close, so fucking close.

"Then come for me," he commands. "Come like the dirty little slut you are."

He gives me one final spank and the impact sends me tumbling in ecstasy. The orgasm hits with a brutal force, and I scream as the rapture crashes over me. My arms give out and I collapse face-first onto the bed.

"Good slut." He rubs the reddened skin of my ass, soothing away the sting. His touch is gentle and I sigh in bliss. I'm not sure I even need any more, this is amazing right now.

"You took that so well. Now for your reward." He pushes me onto my back and spreads my legs again as he settles between them. I feel the heat of his breath before his tongue makes contact, a slow lick from my pussy to my clit. My hips jerk upward. Oh fuck, I didn't expect him to go down on me.

"You taste incredible." His words vibrate against my sensitive flesh. His tongue delves deeper, circling my clit before plunging into me. I moan as my thighs begin to shake.

"Don't you dare come yet," he pulls back just enough to warn me before diving back in. His mouth is relentless—sucking, licking, devouring. When he stops again, his face glistens with my wetness. "Little fucktoys can't come unless they're given permission."

Jesus, it's like this guy walked straight out of one of my fantasies. I fist the sheets, teetering on the edge, but he slows down just as the pressure builds. He circles my clit with his tongue again, light and teasing, before he sucks it hard. Pleasure cascades through me and all I can do is moan.

"So fucking desperate to come," he murmurs. "But you're not going to, are you? Not until I say so."

He alternates between slow, torturous licks and deep, probing thrusts of his tongue. Each movement pushes me closer to bliss. I'm trembling, the tension coiling tighter and tighter.

"Please. Oh god, please." I can hear how needy I sound.

He chuckles. "Please what? Does the fucktoy want to come?"

"Please," I whimper, and rock against his face.

He responds by sucking my clit harder, his fingers digging into my thighs to hold me in place. The ecstasy is almost unbearable, but he doesn't let up.

"Not yet," he growls before moving his tongue faster. "You're going to wait. You're going to take everything I give you."

He pulls away again right as I'm about to shatter. My body aches with need, and I mewl in frustration.

"Now it's my turn." Nick rises and drags me to the end of the mattress, hooking my ankles over his shoulders. He pauses with the tip of his cock poised at my entrance.

"Beg," he commands.

My head is fuzzy as I try to do what he wants. "Please—."

The word is barely out before he's inside me with a brutal thrust. I sob from the sweet burn as he tunnels as deep as he can go.

He withdraws and slams into me again. "Is this what you want?"

"Yes—fuck. Use me," I gasp.

He grins. "Since you asked so nicely."

His pace is punishing and the bedframe rattles. I claw at the bedding, desperate for something to anchor me as I flop around like a rag doll.

"You're just a cum-hungry filthy slut," he growls. "Admit it."

"I'm—fuck—" I cry out as I explode. The orgasm is white-hot and vicious. All coherent thought scatters from my head, and my back arches off the bed.

He doesn't stop, and growls, "Try again. Say it like you mean it."

The words stick in my throat, caught between shame and desire. But the way he's looking at me—like he sees every nasty thought I've ever had—breaks something open inside me.

"I'M A FILTHY SLUT!" I scream. My voice cracks on the last syllable, and when I look over at my husband, his eyes are wide with surprise and lust.

Nick lowers my legs and pulls out, dragging me up towards the headboard. I reach for him instinctively while my body buzzes.

He shakes his head, and orders, "Hands above your head. Keep them there."

I obey, my arms shaking as I grip the headboard. Nick climbs on top of me and slides inside my pussy again. He's fucking me at a different angle now, and he's hitting that perfect spot. My vision blurs, and I come again, my pussy clenching around him.

"Fuck, so tight," he groans and then captures my lips in a demanding kiss.

I moan into his mouth, matching my rhythm to his. When he breaks off the kiss, his gaze locks with mine as he continues to thrust into me. It's so damn dirty to be staring into the eyes of someone not my husband, and it's almost more intimate than having his cock inside me.

His pace is unhurried, drawing out my pleasure, making me feel every inch of him. My orgasm is building again and I'm not going to be able to hold it back.

He holds himself up with one arm as he squeezes my breast and pinches my nipple with his free hand. I moan with every twist of his fingers.

"You're so fucking beautiful." His switch to praise after the degradation is making my head spin. If I was scoring this guy, he'd be off the chart.

Before I can come again, he pulls out and flips me onto my stomach. I let go of the headboard and before I can figure out what's happening, he's inside me again. He slams into me, and the new angle sends shockwaves through me. I clutch the bedding and bury my face in the pillow to muffle my cries.

"Such a good fucktoy," he says, approvingly. "You want my cum?"

"Yes—" I cry out while I shake from another impending orgasm.

"Good slut." His pace slows for a moment. "But first, you're going to come for me again."

I mewl frantically, my muscles already tightening. Nick slides his hand under me, finding my clit. He rubs it, and the sensation is too much. I erupt and cry out as the world fades away. Pure delight assaults me, and I'm transported to another realm where only pleasure exists.

He doesn't stop fucking me, and slams into me with renewed force. I glance over my shoulder, catching sight of my husband sitting in the chair across the room. There's agonized lust in his expression. He's going to need some attention when Nick is done with me.

Nick catches my glance. "You like that, don't you? You like having an audience."

"Yes. Love it!"

Nick keeps his hands on my hips, holding me in place as he pounds into me. The bedframe creaks in unison with the sound of our skin slapping together.

"Where do you want me to come?" The strain in his voice tells me he's close.

Oh god, I get to choose? There's only one place I want it.

"Inside me, please," I beg.

Nick buries himself to the hilt. "Here it comes."

His cock throbs, and he groans as he shoots hot jets of cum deep inside me. I clench around him, milking every last drop, my pussy greedy for all of it. He's trembling from his orgasm as he collapses beside me. We lie there for a few moments and I assume we're done, but he rolls me onto my back. He opens my legs, spreading my pussy lips wide, and giving my husband a direct line of sight to my well-used pussy.

"Look at this mess." Nick traces my pussy with his fingers, and the warmth of his cum begins to drip out. "Fuck, you really took a lot. Such a good little slut."

I bite my lip, trying to hold back a moan, but it escapes anyway.

"Jack, come see what your fucktoy looks like when she's been filled with my cum."

My husband moves closer, studying my pussy, and I imagine Nick is coaxing thick, white fluid to drip out. A tremor runs through me, part embarrassment, part arousal. This is the hottest thing I've done in my life and it makes me feel gloriously slutty.

"Does it turn you on, knowing I fucked you so hard you can't hold it all in?"

Nick's fingers are slippery with his cum as he rubs my clit. My pussy twitches from delight as he presses on the swollen bud.

"Say it," he demands. "Tell me how much you love being a cumdumpster whose only job is to get her holes filled."

Oh fuck. My brain blips out and I gasp, lifting my ass off the bed as I seek more friction. "I love it. Want all the cum."

He smirks, his fingers sliding into my pussy to gather more of his cum. He brings his wet fingers to my mouth. "Tell me how good my cum tastes."

I open my mouth, and he slides his fingers inside, coating my tongue. The salty, musky flavor fills my senses and I can taste both of us on his skin. I swirl my tongue around his fingers before sucking them clean.

He removes his fingers from my mouth and I sigh, "So fucking good."

Nick's lips brush my ear. "That's right. You're a perfect little fucktoy. Now, let's see if I can make you beg for more."

My mind is a tangle of pleasure and submission, and I'm ready for whatever comes next.

An hour later, I'm bent over the desk in the main room. My hair is wrapped around Nick's fist as he yanks my head back. He whacks into my pussy from behind while the desk creaks. The mirror on the wall in front of me reflects a woman who has been fucked hard—lipstick smeared, lips puffy from brutal kisses, hair wild.

"Look at yourself," he growls. "Look at what a fucking slut you are for this."

I am looking at a slut. I'm looking at me. My fingers grip the sides of the desk as I push back to meet his thrusts. I want to come one more time.

"Harder," I demand. "Fuck me like you mean it."

He chuckles, "You do like it rough," and obliges. His grip on my hair tightens and each thrust is punishing.

"Yes." I'm aching for more. "Don't hold back."

He doesn't. He pounds into me furiously as the desk shakes. I'm close to another orgasm and this one is going to be massive. He pins my shoulder to the desk, changing the angle of his thrust, and my orgasm blasts through me. It's intense and overwhelming, and I can't tell if I'm screaming or begging for more. He keeps fucking me through my orgasm and I can tell he's beyond reason. He's about to come again, and I'm lost in a sea of pleasure, drowning in pure bliss as bolts of ecstasy ripple through my entire body.

His body tenses and he lets out a guttural sound before slamming into me one last time. He shudders, his cock pulsing as he fills me with another load of sticky cum. I can feel the wetness spreading inside me, and it sends another rush of pleasure coursing through my veins.

For a moment, we stay like that, our bodies locked together. He releases my hair before pulling out, and when I try to stand up, my legs are like Jell-O. Jack is immediately at my side, scooping me up and sitting down in the nearest chair to cuddle me.

"Holy shit," Jack murmurs, and I can hear the awe in his voice.

Nick groans as he sprawls on the couch across from us. "Okay, I'm going to feel this tomorrow."

I have to hold in a giggle and Jack's chest moves like he's trying not to laugh. Yeah, I'm going to be achy tomorrow too. So amazing.

"Jack, I hope you got your money's worth." Nick's comment almost makes me laugh again.

"Oh, I sure did. That was great."

My husband cock is hard through his jeans. Yeah, he definitely liked the show.

Nick grins at us. "Well, I'm glad I could provide such satisfactory service."

The men talk about the resort and gambling as I regain my composure, and with Jack's help, I get dressed.

"I'm going to take Holly back to my room," Jack says. "Thanks for everything, Nick."

Nick looks exhausted and happy. "It was great meeting you, Holly."

"Thank you. This was exactly what I needed," I reply, and revel in how naughty it is to say goodbye to a guy I just fucked, knowing I won't see him again.

As soon as we're in the hallway and the door closes behind us, my husband's patience drops. He tugs me towards the elevator and I giggle. Oh yeah, he needs me.

CHAPTER 5

We barely make it into our hotel room before he's all over me. Once the door clicks shut behind us, Jack whirls me around, pressing my back against the hotel wall. His lips latch onto mine, insistent. I moan at the familiar taste of him. It's comforting after the intense encounter. His hands roam over my body, tracing the curves he knows so well, igniting fresh flames of desire.

He whispers, "I can't wait. I need to feel you, all of you."

I reach for his belt, fumbling with the buckle in my haste. He helps me, shoving his jeans and boxers down just enough to free his cock. I grasp him and give a little squeeze.

He groans, "Fuck, Holly. You drive me crazy."

When he lifts me up, my dress rides up as I wrap my legs around his waist. He pushes my panties aside, and in one swift movement, he's inside me. I'm a little tender but his cock feels different...better. He fucks me with my back against the wall, and each thrust makes me gasp.

"Jack." My fingers dig into his shoulders. "Harder!"

He hammers me into the wall. I'm almost afraid I won't come before he does, but as soon as he shudders with his release, the thought of his cum mixing with Nick's skyrockets me into bliss.

My orgasm doesn't just crash over me—it detonates. Every nerve in my body ignites at once, like someone's set off a thousand tiny fireworks under my skin. Ecstasy rips through me, and I clench around him, my pussy pulsing in waves. Fuck, fuck, fuck. I can't think–can't do anything but feel.

He groans as he pumps me full of cum. Each spurt gives me another rush of pleasure until I'm shaking from the high. When we can move again, he carries me over to the bed, laying me down gently, but I'm still reeling. Holy shit. That was something else.

I look up at him, and his expression is soft and filled with love. He kisses me softly. "I love you."

"I love you too, babe."

Tonight was beyond anything I imagined, and I feel a completeness I didn't expect. I breathe in the scent of sex on my husband and giggle. "I'm glad we did this."

He pulls me close. "Me too. Seeing you licking his cum off your finger s..."

He shudders and his cock hardens. Holy fuck, again?

This time, he takes it slow and removes all our clothes. As he makes love to me, it's like he's trying to remind me of why we work so well together. He knows my body almost better than I know myself, and it's just one continual surge of bliss. When I finally peak, it's a mind-numbing orgasm that leaves me limp.

And in the tangled aftermath, I know two things. The first is that I would do this all again.

I smile to myself. The second is that we WILL do this all again.

The End

HOTWIFE FOR THE SPRING

A FIRST TIME HOTWIFE STORY

LACEY CROSS

CHAPTER 1

I'm supposed to be reading my book club selection—some literary masterpiece about a woman finding herself through artisanal cheese-making—but instead I'm conducting what I like to call "field research" from my weathered Adirondack chair on the deck. The book lies forgotten in my lap as I watch two exceedingly attractive men attack the woodpile behind our rented lake house.

My husband Devon approaches each log with methodical precision, all controlled power and perfect form. Meanwhile, his best friend Jason has apparently confused wood-chopping with some primal display, throwing his whole body into each swing like he's auditioning for a lumberjack calendar.

Or maybe he's just performing for me.

"You know," I call out, not bothering to hide my appreciation, "most women have to pay good money for this kind of entertainment."

Jason pauses mid-swing, shooting me a grin that's pure trouble. "What's the going rate these days?"

"Keep chopping and maybe we'll negotiate."

Devon laughs, never breaking rhythm. "Careful, Kristy drives a hard bargain."

"I bet she does." Jason's eyes lock with mine for a beat too long before he returns to his log. "Good thing I like a challenge."

My dress suddenly feels too tight in the cool afternoon breeze. I pretend to read, but my attention keeps drifting to them—two men, two very different rhythms as they work. They're chopping wood so we can enjoy a fire later; the nights still bite this early in the season. I never imagined the flex and swing of their muscles would be so captivating... or so wildly distracting.

I flip a page without absorbing a single word. The cheese lady will have to wait—I'm busy pretending I'm the suburban equivalent of a wildlife documentarian.

Here we observe the domestic husband in his natural habitat, wielding primitive tools while his mate watches from a strategically-positioned chair...

"You're staring again," Devon says without looking up.

"Can you blame me? It's not every day I get a front row seat to watch two men doing manly outdoor shit."

"We've been at this for thirty minutes." Jason pauses to wipe sweat from his brow with the back of his hand.

"Mmm, yes you have." I settle into the chair, letting the hem of my dress ride up as I cross my legs. I don't bother adjusting the fabric. "Thirty minutes of pure educational value."

Jason's gaze flickers to the exposed skin of my thighs before returning to his task. That brief glance sends warmth spiraling through me.

Devon notices the glance between us. This whole weekend is his brainchild—months of boundary-setting and what-if talks distilled into a lake-house escape with Devon's oldest friend. Newly divorced, Jason knows we've been toying with the idea of my stepping into hotwife territory. We trust him, and Jason says he's more than willing to be part of my first experience—if I choose to go through with it. The decision is entirely mine.

"Almost done here," Devon announces, embedding his axe in the chopping block. "Getting hungry?"

My pulse quickens. He has no idea. "Starving, actually. Plus you two are ruining my concentration." I fan myself with the book. "How's a girl supposed to focus on artisanal cheese when there's all this artisanal masculinity on display?"

"Did you just compare us to cheese?" Devon laughs, climbing the porch steps.

"Premium cheese," I correct with a wicked smile. "Aged to perfection. Like fine forty-something men should be."

Jason joins us, axe slung over his shoulder like he stepped out of a fantasy. "I don't know whether to be flattered or offended at being compared to dairy products in our early forties."

"Definitely flattered." I let my eyes travel slowly up his frame. "Trust me. Some things just get better with age."

"So what's for lunch?" Jason's voice is casual, but based on the growing evidence in his pants, I can tell I'm getting to him. "All this hard labor's worked up quite an appetite."

Devon answers before I can. "Burgers. Unless Kristy's hungry for something else."

I can think of plenty of things I'm hungry for. Even though I'm not the one who thought up this plan, I'm finding myself warming up to the idea of becoming a hotwife.

Jason sets the axe down and stretches, muscles shifting beneath tanned skin. My mouth goes dry, and I'm tempted to fan myself again. Oh yeah, things are getting very, *very* warm.

"Burgers sound perfect," I manage, though part of me wants to make a joke about preferring sausage. I restrain myself—barely.

Devon and I agreed today would be about comfort and chemistry, testing the waters. The strategic shirtless wood-chopping was probably no accident.

But I know how to play this game. This dress wasn't a random choice either.

"I'll fire up the grill," Jason offers.

Devon wiggles his eyebrows at me. "And I'll grab the meat."

I groan. "You're about as subtle as a freight train."

"Says the woman who's been eye-fucking us for the past hour."

"Thirty minutes," I correct primly. "And it's not my fault you two decided to reenact the opening scene of a porno."

The men laugh, and as Jason goes into the house, Devon leans over me and kisses my temple. "Jason's been watching you all morning. That dress was tactical brilliance."

A flush runs through my body, and I'm pleased my outfit is working as intended. The spring green fabric is my secret weapon—innocent enough, but clingy in all the right places. Plus, I'm not wearing a bra or panties, which makes every movement feel naughty.

Devon heads inside, and I follow him in. Despite my flirtiness, I'm still uncertain if I can go through with this. The fantasy version of being a hotwife is one thing. The reality of fucking them at the same time is something else entirely... because Devon doesn't want to just watch, he wants to participate.

Once the grill is ready, Devon does his manly meat tending, and Jason hangs with me on the deck.

"So," he says. "Do you really want this?"

Oh no, is he trying to back out? I don't want him to change his mind right when I decide to go for it. "Are you having second thoughts?"

"Not a single one." He regards me with an intensity that sends a shiver of pleasure through me. "Just making sure we're all on the same page."

"The page where my husband and his best friend want me? And where I want them? Yeah, we're on that page."

At least, I believe we are. The slutty version of me absolutely is. She's highlighted and dog-eared that page. The real me is still catching up.

Jason laughs. "You've always been direct. It's one of the things I've always liked about you."

"One of the things?"

"The list is extensive." His eyes drop to my exposed cleavage. "And growing."

If he keeps looking at me that way, I'm going to combust. "We should go fix a plate. The meat should be done soon," I say, my voice betraying me with a slight tremor.

I turn to go into the house, but Jason's words stop me. "Just so we're clear. I've wanted this—wanted you—for years."

My brain goes haywire and I face him. "How many years?"

"Remember that Fourth of July party? You in that red bikini?"

That was a very memorable night, and I do a quick calculation. "That was at least twelve years ago."

"Yes, and I watched Devon fuck you behind the boathouse while everyone else was watching fireworks."

The revelation hits me like lightning. "You saw us?"

"Not on purpose. I was drunk and looking for the bathroom. I was afraid to disturb you and ruin the moment."

The image of Jason hidden in the shadows while Devon fucked me against the wall, sends liquid heat pooling between my thighs. Fuck, that's hot.

"Did you touch yourself?" I whisper.

"Later. In the shower. Thinking about how you looked when you came."

"Jesus, Jason—"

"Burgers are ready," Devon calls, interrupting the moment.

Jason smiles. "Guess we eat."

My legs feel unsteady as I follow him to the grill. The knowing look my husband gives me says he can tell I'm flustered, and approves.

"Am I going to need to hose you two down so you can cool off?" Devon jokes.

"I was confessing to Kristy about how I saw you guys fucking at the Fourth of July party years ago," Jason replies.

Devon laughs. "Oh yeah, that."

I almost squeak in shock. Devon KNEW and he didn't tell me? As we make our way into the house, I try to decide if I would have even wanted to know. I probably would have died of embarrassment every time I saw Jason, while simultaneously being turned on, so I'll forgive him for keeping it from me.

We eat on the porch and the conversation flows easily. Twenty years of friendship between the guys, and fifteen years since I met Jason, means we never run out of things to discuss.

"Should we take the boat out?" Devon suggests as we finish eating. "The weather's beautiful."

"I'm game," Jason nods. "Been too long since I've been on the water."

I stand to gather the plates. "I'll clean up and meet you down there."

Jason catches my wrist as I reach for his empty plate. "Leave it. I'll help later."

His thumb traces circles on my pulse point.

"Okay," I agree, my voice embarrassingly breathy.

Suddenly I imagine lying down on the picnic table, spreading my legs, and telling the boys to "come and get it." Yeah, that isn't really me.

Devon watches our exchange with heated interest. "I'll grab the cooler. Jason, there's life vests in the shed."

As they head off to prepare the boat, I take a moment to steady myself. After months of planning we're finally here.

I just have to be brave enough to take what they're offering.

Chapter 2

I don't change my dress. Why would I? It's working exactly as intended, and I haven't even flashed the guys yet.

Here we observe the suburban wife employing the ancient mating ritual of strategic wardrobe selection. Notice how the specimen contemplates "accidentally" dropping items to give the male species a peek at her lady bits.

I giggle to myself in the bathroom mirror as I put my hair in a ponytail. Yep, I look great—casual and sexy.

As I walk to the docks, Jason is stowing the lifejackets in the storage compartment of the boat while Devon loads the cooler.

"Operation Threesome is a go," I say to myself. At least I hope it's a go, once my brain stops overanalyzing everything.

The men turn as I approach, and I give them my best sultry tone. "I'm ready for adventure."

The lake smells like spring and there are no other boats out on the water. I sit at the back while Jason takes the middle rowing bench facing me, and Devon sits in the front. The boat creaks with each pull of the oars. It's peaceful.

The rowboat isn't big, and I stretch my arms up in the air. Giving the breeze a chance to create a strategic wardrobe malfunction, I open my legs a tiny bit, and the hem of my dress lifts just enough to flash my inner thighs. When Jason's knuckles go white on the oars, it bolsters my confidence.

Devon can't see what I'm doing that easily, but he sees Jason tense up, so he jokes, "Is my wife flashing you?"

My body tingles at his possessive tone. He's been using the words 'my wife,' a lot today, as if he's willing to share me, but he's making it clear who I belong to. I can have some fun with this.

"Don't be jealous." I peek over Jason's shoulder at him. "You get to see this view whenever you want."

"Uh...her dress is having some difficulty staying in place," Jason says.

Jason seems flustered as he tries to row and not stare at my legs. His reaction makes me feel powerful... sexy. I purr at him, "But do you like the view?"

"Like you have to ask." Jason laughs.

I deliberately look at the bulge in his jeans. "You're right. I don't."

I'm enjoying the freedom to let whatever slutty thought I have come out of my mouth. I usually have to muzzle this side of myself in public.

I shift in my seat, letting the neckline gape. A bead of sweat trickles between my breasts, and I don't miss how Jason tracks its path.

"Remember in college when we spent that weekend at the lake?" Jason says suddenly.

Oh god, I had just recently started dating Devon and I was definitely a free spirit back then.

Devon replies, "Yeah, when Kristy insisted on skinny dipping and nearly gave that fishing boat of retirees a heart attack."

I roll my eyes. "They were at least fifty yards away."

"They had binoculars," Jason points out.

"For bird watching."

"Well, you gave them something else to watch that day," Jason teases.

"I was a bit reckless back then," I say, the memory flickering between us. We were drunk on cheap beer and the freedom of youth. I stripped down while these two pretended not to look. But I knew they were watching, and I loved every second of it.

"And now?"

Jason's question makes my stomach flip. Is he asking if I'm reckless and ready to cross this line?

I glance at Devon, finding reassurance in his expression. Then back to Jason, whose eyes hold newly-acknowledged desire.

I occasionally watch motivational speeches online, and one I saw recently had a line that spoke to me: "The bravest decisions happen in the spaces between thoughts."

Fuck it. It's time to take what I really want.

I sit up straight and slide the thin straps of my sundress down my arms, baring my breasts to the open air.

"Holy fuck," Jason breathes, and the oars slip, one almost sliding from his hands entirely.

"Something distracting you?" I say, and my voice isn't as steady as I'd like.

"You could say that." Jason's gaze is fixed on my breasts, and my nipples pucker as desire simmers in my core.

Devon must like what I'm doing because he says, "Show him what he's been missing, baby."

Heat flares through me at his words. I'm suddenly aware this isn't a private lake.

"What if someone sees?" I ask, not really caring.

I feel gloriously filthy.

"Then they get a free show," Devon says. "But I think they'd need binoculars."

"Bird watchers," Jason and I say in unison, then laugh.

The carefree moment loosens something inside me and I lean towards Jason, thankful that this isn't a large boat. I put my hands on his thighs for balance. The bulge in his jeans has gotten larger, and I run my hand over it, feeling his cock jump beneath my touch.

"So this is happening?" he asks.

I grin at him. "Unless you want me to stop."

"Fuck no."

He nests the oars back into their locks, freeing his hands. He caresses my shoulders and then finds the end of my ponytail, giving it a slow, playful twirl.

I undo the button on his jeans, and drag down his zipper, freeing his cock from his boxers. It's huge—thicker than Devon's. Fuck, if my husband had told me what Jason was packing, I might not have hesitated. This is going to be fun, assuming Jason knows how to use it.

"So tiny," I muse.

Jason barks a laugh that turns into a groan as I take him in my mouth. He's salty and has a different taste from my husband. I sink down, taking him deeper.

"Jesus Christ," he hisses. "Your mouth."

I slowly pull off him, his shaft glistening with my saliva. When I look up, his gaze is molten with hunger. "Tell me..." I trace his shaft with my fingertips, "does watching me worship your cock turn you on?"

"Fuck yes," he says. "You look so fucking hot with your lips around me."

"She loves it," Devan says, and his filthy words thrill me as I suck on Jason again. "She loves being a little slut for cock."

Jason groans, "Is that what you are? A little slut for my cock?"

Fuck, I don't know why I enjoy it when Devon talks to me like this, and Jason joining in makes my head whirl. I moan around him, the vibration making him shudder. I stop sucking and whisper, "Yes."

"Say it," Jason demands. "Tell me you're a slut for my cock."

"I'm a slut for your cock." Hearing myself admit to being a slut for a cock that isn't my husband's sinks me further into my role, my body thrumming with submission.

Devon's voice is a low rumble of approval. "That's it, baby. Show him what a good little fucktoy you are."

I go back to sucking on Jason's cock. His moans fill the air, mixed with the lapping of the water against the boat. Even though I chose to do this, it still feels like I'm being used, and the thought sends a surge of wetness to my pussy.

"Fuck, your mouth is unbelievable," Jason pants and he wraps my ponytail around his fist and guides my head up and down on his shaft.

My eyes water as he hits the back of my throat. The boat rocks gently beneath us, adding to the eroticism of the moment.

"Remember when we caught that Mets game?" Jason says, his voice strained. "You two in the bathroom stall? I heard Devon fucking you. I jerked off thinking about how much you loved it."

I remove his cock from my mouth, and my lips feel swollen and slick. "You heard us?"

"You weren't exactly quiet." Jason grins. "I could hear every moan. It drove me crazy."

Devon laughs. "Trust me, she's never quiet."

"Something to look forward to then," Jason says, and then groans when I continue sucking on him. "Your mouth is better than I imagined."

"You imagined this?" I pull back again to ask, my lips brushing against the tip of his cock as I speak.

"Only about a thousand times."

That confession sends another bolt of heat through me. I hollow my cheeks as I suck him hard for a moment before tracing my tongue along the underside and ask, "How many times have you touched yourself while thinking about me?"

"Too many to count." His hips flex as I sink my lips all the way to the base of his shaft. "Fuck, I'm gonna—"

His body tenses, and he explodes in my mouth, his cum is bitter, but not unpleasant. I swallow every drop, my throat working to take it all.

When he's finally finished, he drags in a ragged breath and looks at me in awe. "Well, that was worth the twelve-year wait."

I lick my lips, tasting him still. "We'll have even more fun when we get back to the house."

Devon laughs, the sound proud and full of lust. "I've created a monster."

My body throbs with desire. "Pretty sure I was always like this. You just gave me permission to show it."

"And a willing accomplice," Jason adds, tucking himself away with hands that aren't quite steady. "Let's go back," he says, taking up the oars again. "Before someone really does come by with binoculars."

I pull up the top of my dress, my nipples hard and sensitive against the fabric. I watch Jason as he rows, the muscles in his forearms flexing with each stroke. Sweat glistens on his brow, and his t-shirt clings to him.

Two men. One weekend.

And we've barely started. I can't wait to see what other trouble we can get up to.

Chapter 3

My legs tremble when we step off the boat. The dock sways beneath my feet—or maybe that's just me, unsteady from what happened on the water.

"Careful there," Jason says as he holds my arm. "Wouldn't want you falling in after all that effort."

I can just imagine what I look like right now. Lips swollen, hair mussed, the taste of him still lingering on my tongue–like I just got run over by the Lust Bus.

"I think I forgot how to think," I mutter, which makes Devon grin.

Here we observe the thoroughly slutty suburban wife, attempting to maintain dignity while the taste of cum lingers in her mouth. A fascinating specimen in all her glory.

"You good?" Devon asks, his thumb tracing circles at the small of my back.

"I'm spectacular," I reply, finding my balance. "Just trying to remember how legs work."

Jason laughs. "If your legs don't work now, just wait until later."

"Is that a threat or a promise?" I ask, raising an eyebrow.

He drops his voice an octave. "Definitely a promise." The low tone sends a fresh zing of heat between my thighs.

The walk back to the house feels endless. Every step reminds me of what just happened, of Jason's cock in my mouth, of Devon watching. I'm ready for more.

"Anyone want some water?" Devon asks as we reach the porch steps. "You two should probably hydrate after that...workout."

"God, yes," I say, at the same time Jason says, "Absolutely."

Inside, the cabin feels different—charged, expectant.

"So," I say, leaning a hip against the kitchen counter. "That happened."

"Any regrets?" Jason asks, and there's a hint of vulnerability beneath his casual tone.

"Only that we waited so long," I admit, accepting a glass of water from Devon. The cool liquid feels refreshing after the heat of what we did on the boat.

Jason grins and takes a long drink. "Yeah, and now I'm pretty sure I need to update my bucket list."

"Riiight," I snort.

"'Watch Kristy give world-class head,'" he says without missing a beat. "Check."

I nearly choke on my water. "You did not have that on your actual bucket list."

"You're right," Jason says, completely serious. "It's more specific. It says, 'Watch Kristy give world-class head while looking absolutely gorgeous doing it."

Devon laughs. "Smooth, man. Real smooth."

"Apparently I need to work on my bucket list game," I say, wiping water from my chin.

Jason takes a drink and his throat works as he swallows. The movement draws my attention to the strong column of his neck, the shadow of stubble along his jaw. God, he's gorgeous. I flash back to his cock in my mouth and the weight of him on my tongue. He's attractive and he has a big cock—a combination that makes my insides clench in protest since I've yet to get a cock inside me today.

"You're staring again," Jason points out, his lip quirking up in a sexy half-smile.

"Just admiring the view." I don't bother hiding my appreciation. Why should I? We're past pretending.

Devon sets his glass down and moves behind me, placing his hands on my hips. I press against him, feeling his erection against my ass.

"You know what I've been thinking about?" he whispers in my ear, loud enough for Jason to hear.

I shimmy my hips to brush against his cock. "Mmm, what's that?"

"How you'd look between us..." He kisses my earlobe, making me shiver. "While we fuck you at the same time."

"Jesus, Devon." The water glass nearly slips from my grasp, so I set it on the counter with a shaky hand. The mental image of them surrounding me and inside me makes my knees weak.

There's a hungry expression on Jason's face as he watches Devon's hands roam over my body. "I've been thinking the same thing."

"Great minds," Devon says with a wicked grin.

I look between them. Two smoking hot men who want me with an intensity that's dizzying. "So what're you waiting for?"

"Not a damn thing," Jason says, closing the distance between us in two strides.

He kisses me slowly, like he's memorizing the shape of my mouth. His tongue slides against mine as Devon, still behind me, pushes the straps of my dress down my shoulders.

"Been thinking about this all day." Devon kisses along my neck as the dress falls to my waist.

Jason's hands bracket my ribs, thumbs just brushing the undersides of my breasts. He breaks the kiss to look down at my exposed chest. "So gorgeous."

"I've been telling her that for years," Devon says, cupping my breasts and playing with my nipples. "She still acts surprised every time."

I would protest that it's not *every* time, but the pleasure of four hands on my body short-circuits my brain. Devon removes his hands so Jason can take over, rolling my nipples between his fingers. Bliss swirls in my core and I'm desperate for more.

"This is unfair," I moan, my head falling back against Devon's shoulder. "I'm the only one naked."

"Half-naked," Devon corrects, tugging the dress down over my hips until it pools at my feet. "Now that's better."

I stand completely bare between them, skin flushed with arousal.

"My point stands," I say, reaching for the hem of Jason's shirt. "Too many clothes on you guys."

They undress quickly, and I admire how sexy they are together–Devon's familiar body, lean and strong, and Jason's broader frame, his chest dusted with hair that narrows to a trail leading to his impressive cock.

Soon we're rushing towards the bedroom in a laughing jumble. Jason's hands cup my ass as Devon leads the way, pausing occasionally to kiss me.

"Watch the side table," Devon warns, steering me around a corner.

"I'm a little distracted here," I moan, as Jason's hand slides between my legs from behind, finding the slick evidence of my arousal.

"I can tell," Jason says. "You're soaked."

His fingers circle my entrance, teasing but not penetrating, driving me crazy.

We finally make it into the bedroom and tumble onto the king-size bed in a breathless tangle, limbs and laughter everywhere. I end up pinned between them—Devon sprawled beneath me, Jason molded to my back. The heat of their skin against mine feels like being wrapped in living fire.

"How do you want this?" Devon asks as he tweaks a nipple, making me gasp.

My body vibrates with need. I trust them both completely. They could do whatever they want to me, and I would love it. "Every way possible."

"Ambitious," Jason laughs.

"We have all weekend," I remind him. "But right now, I want one of you in my pussy and the other in my ass."

Devon's cock twitches against my thigh. "You sure?"

"Mmm hmm." I nod, wiggling against him. "I need your cocks before I go crazy."

Jason reaches for the lube on the nightstand. Devon must have conveniently set it there earlier. Devon positions me above him, the head of his cock nudging the entrance of my pussy. I watch his face as I sink onto him with a whimper.

Devon grasps my hips. "Fuck, baby."

I'm extra sensitive and even though this is my husband's cock, somehow today it feels different—more intense, more forbidden with Jason watching, waiting his turn. I lean forward and Jason uses lube and works me open carefully.

"Breathe," he says, kissing along my shoulder blades. "Just relax."

The dual sensation overwhelms me—Devon inside me, Jason's fingers opening me up, both of them murmuring encouragement. I feel split open, exposed and vulnerable, and yet completely safe between them.

"Ready?" Jason asks.

"Yes," I moan, and Devon's hands on my waist hold me steady as the head of Jason's cock presses where his fingers just were.

"Oh god," I gasp as he pushes in slowly, the stretch burning in a delicious way. My body resists at first, then yields, accepting him inch by inch.

"Fuck," Jason moans. "So good."

Devon cups my face, bringing my attention back to him. His eyes search mine for any sign of discomfort. "You okay, sweetheart?"

"Yes, don't stop," I pant out for both their benefit as my body adjusts to the overwhelming fullness.

They fuck me, finding a pleasurable rhythm that makes flashes of light twinkle at the corners of my vision. The sensation defies description—the friction between them creates a pressure that builds with each thrust, an ecstasy I couldn't have imagined. My toes curl as the rapture builds in layers.

"So fucking good," Devon says and lifts his hips to meet me.

Jason increases his pace, his hands gripping my shoulders. "You have no idea how long I've dreamed about this."

I'm beyond coherent thought, reduced to sensation and need. Every nerve ending zings from pleasure, and I mewl desperately as bliss rushes through me.

"Oh fuck. Oh fuck." I'm chanting a continuous stream as I slam down on Devon's cock in time with Jason's thrusts into my ass. My body is no longer my own—it belongs to them, to this moment, to the pleasure that threatens to tear me apart.

"She's close," Devon tells Jason, sliding his hand between my legs to brush circles around my clit. "Aren't you, baby?"

"Yes," I gasp, teetering on the edge. "Please. I need it."

Jason's thrusts become more forceful. "Then come for us."

Devon's fingers speed up on my clit, and that's all it takes to send me hurtling over the abyss. My orgasm zings through me with stunning force, my body clenching around both of them as I cry out. Waves of pleasure radiate outward from my core, my vision blurring as every muscle contracts.

"Fuck, she's squeezing us so tight," Jason pants, his rhythm faltering.

"I know," Devon grits out, his hips jerking upward.

They come almost simultaneously. As they flood me with cum, it triggers another ripple of delight, a smaller orgasm that leaves me breathless. For a moment, we're in a frenzy as we take our pleasure from each other.

Then Jason collapses against my back. We lie there, sweat-slicked and trembling, until Jason finally rolls to the side, bringing me with him so we're all sprawled across the bed.

"Holy shit," I whisper after a moment, staring at the ceiling. My body feels like it's been taken apart and put back together differently. "That was..."

"Yeah," Devon agrees, finding my hand on the mattress and squeezing it.

"Fucking incredible," Jason finishes.

We lie in comfortable silence, the only sound our gradually slowing breaths. My body throbs pleasantly. I could get used to this.

"I need a shower," I finally say, making no effort to get up.

"In a minute," Devon mumbles, sounding half-asleep.

Jason props himself up on one elbow, looking down at me with a mixture of satisfaction and wonder. "You're something else, you know that?"

"So I've been told." I trace the line of his jaw with my fingertip, feeling the slight roughness of stubble. "Still worth the twelve-year wait?"

"Worth every fucking second."

Devon rolls onto his side, draping his arm over my waist. "Told you she'd blow your mind."

"Among other things," Jason quips, and our comfortable joking warms me. This feels right, having Jason here with us.

I lie between them, surrounded by warmth and the scent of sex. My body aches in the most pleasant way possible, and I feel utterly, completely satisfied. This is what it feels like to take exactly what you want, I realize. No shame, no hesitation—just pleasure and connection.

"Shower," I insist again, though I still just lie there. "I'm disgusting."

"You're amazing," Devon corrects, and kisses my shoulder.

"Seconded," Jason agrees.

I smile up at the ceiling, utterly content. My limbs feel like rubber, heavy and useless. "I think one of you is going to have to carry me to the bathroom."

"We'll just have to think of the proper incentive to get you up," Devon teases.

"I dunno, I think it's going to take more than you can offer at the moment." I glance down at their spent cocks with a smirk.

Jason sits up. "I'll at least start the water, just in case you find the energy."

As he heads to the bathroom, I turn to look at Devon. "You okay?"

"More than okay. You?"

I'm honest with him. "This was fantastic."

"And the weekend isn't over yet," he reminds me.

From the bathroom comes the sound of running water, and Jason peeks his head out of the door. "Water's hot."

"So are you," I call back, making the guys snicker.

Devon helps me up, steadying me when my legs threaten to give out. "Easy there, champ."

"Your fault," I accuse, leaning into him. "Both of you."

"Guilty as charged," he agrees, leading me into the bathroom.

The shower is barely large enough for three, but we make it work, taking turns under the spray. There's something incredibly intimate about washing each other—Jason's hands working shampoo through my hair, Devon soaping up my back.

"We should do this more often," Jason says as he massages my scalp.

"The threesome or the shower?" I ask, moaning in bliss as his fingers work their magic.

"Both," he and Devon say in unison, and we all laugh.

After, wrapped in towels, we collapse back onto the bed. The sheets are a disaster, but none of us care enough to change them. I curl into Devon's side, Jason sprawled behind me, his palm resting on my hip.

Devon yawns. "Nap, then dinner?"

My eyelids droop. "Just a cat nap."

Jason mumbles something that might be agreement before his breathing evens out.

As I drift off, I think about how I have two men who want nothing more than to pleasure me completely. I'm living my best life.

Our cat nap turns into a full-blown coma until Jason's stomach rumbles loud enough to wake us all. Dinner becomes delivery pizza eaten naked on the porch, the darkness our only cover. I sit between them, innocently minding my own business until Jason smears sauce on my nipple and Devon licks it clean. The night dissolves into a blur of hands and mouths and cocks.

I lose count of how many times I come. On the couch with Jason's cock buried in my pussy. Bent over a kitchen bar stool, Devon pounding into me from behind while I suck Jason off. In the shower, sandwiched between them once more, water cascading down our bodies as they fill me completely.

Sometime around midnight, I wake to Jason's lips on my neck, his hard cock against my ass. "Again?" I whisper, and he just growls in response, sliding into me while Devon watches through half-lidded eyes before joining in.

We finally crash around 3 a.m. with satisfied smiles. My body aches deliciously, used in ways I never imagined. I fall asleep with the taste of them on my tongue, their cum dried on my skin, and completely happy.

Chapter 4

When I wake up the next morning, I'm alone. My body feels deliciously used as I stretch, and I wince at the pleasant ache between my thighs.

I examine the marks they left—a light bruise blooming on my inner thigh, a tender spot on my breast where Jason got a little enthusiastic. Evidence. Souvenirs.

I decide to take a quick shower. I'm sore in the best possible way, like after an intense workout but infinitely more satisfying. My nipples harden under the spray, still sensitive from being pinched and sucked until I begged.

After toweling off, I pull on a pair of cotton shorts and a t-shirt. No bra, no panties. What's the point? We're just going to end up naked again anyway.

I'm drawn to the kitchen by the sound of laughter and the scent of coffee and something sweet. They're making me breakfast. My men. My husband and his best friend, who fucked me senseless last night. Who both want more.

And so do I.

The sight that greets me in the kitchen is straight out of a fantasy—Jason is flipping pancakes at the stove while Devon slices fruit. They're shirtless, sweatpants riding low on their hips, and looking ridiculously sexy doing domestic shit.

Here we observe the suburban wife in her natural habitat, appreciating the fine male specimens on display while suffering mild dehydration from previous mating rituals.

Yeah, okay, I'm silly, and the thought makes me smile.

"Hey, you're awake. You come to find out what's taking breakfast so long?" Devon comments without looking up.

"Mmm, more like to admire the scenery," I reply, crossing to the coffee pot. "Two shirtless men making breakfast? My birthday came early."

Jason slides a plate of blueberry pancakes onto the counter. "After last night, I'd say several things came early."

I groan. "Sex jokes before I've had caffeine should be banned."

"But my wit is just one of my many talents," he replies with a wink that makes my stomach flip.

Devon sets a bowl of sliced strawberries next to the pancakes. "Eat up. You burned a lot of calories yesterday."

"Are we planning to burn more today?" I ask as I load up a plate.

Devon's smile turns wicked. "That depends."

"On what?"

"On how well you beg."

The challenge in his voice sends heat straight between my legs. I take a sip of my coffee and purr at him, "I'll beg like you've never seen me beg before."

Jason makes a sound somewhere between a laugh and a groan. "Now this I've gotta see."

We eat quickly, as if we all agree we want to be tangled up together as soon as possible.

When I keep peeking at Jason, he licks syrup from his thumb, and says, "You keep looking at my mouth."

"Just thinking about where I'd like it to be."

Devon joins in. "I think you should tell us in great detail exactly where that would be."

I stand, stretching to make my shirt ride up. "Why don't I show you instead?"

They exchange a look that makes my pulse quicken—a silent communication that says they're about to wreck me.

"Lead the way," Jason says, and stands up.

Instead of heading towards the bedroom, I go into the living room and stand in front of the large picture window that overlooks the lake.

"Here," I decide, pulling my shirt over my head.

Devon moves in front of me and tilts my head up for a kiss that's tender and possessive.

"You're fucking magnificent," he murmurs against my lips.

Jason presses against my back. "Anyone on the lake could see us," he points out, though he doesn't sound concerned.

"Let them watch," I reply, reaching for him. "I'm not feeling shy today."

He laughs. "Clearly."

Devon's hands slide down my back while Jason pushes my shorts down to the floor. The contrast between the two men makes me shiver—Devon's touch is familiar and confident, while Jason's is exploratory, like he can't believe he has permission to do this.

"Tell us what you want," Devon commands.

I don't really care as long as their mouths are on me, and I say, "You can start by kissing my neck."

"She likes it when you nibble right here," Devon says as he kisses the sensitive spot on my neck.

I gasp as Jason follows his lead on the opposite side, teeth grazing my skin with just the right pressure.

"What else does she like?" Jason asks.

Devon slides his hand between my legs, cupping my pussy. "She likes to be fingered while her nipples are sucked."

"Like this?" Jason asks, his mouth closing around my nipple as Devon finger fucks me.

Oh god, that feels so good. I moan, "Exactly like that."

They work me over until I'm vibrating with pleasure. I'm about ready to beg someone to fuck me when Devon guides me over to the couch and applies pressure to my shoulders until I sit. Before I can even process what is happening, Devon spreads my legs and kneels between them.

I arch my back as he holds my pussylips open and feasts. Jason sits close to me and immediately sucks on a nipple again.

"She's a tasty dessert," Devon announces, his breath a warm puff of air against my sensitive flesh.

"Less talk, more licking," I demand and press his head back to my pussy. When he growls and enthusiastically nuzzles me, I half laugh and half moan as each flick of his tongue shoots bliss through me.

They work in sync, Devon's fingers in my pussy and his tongue on my clit, while Jason sucks on my breasts. I can hear myself gasping and moaning, but I'm not saying anything intelligible. They're frying my brain with pleasure.

"She's close," Devon murmurs. "Her thighs are trembling."

Jason lifts his head and studies my face with fascination. "I want to watch her come."

Devon's fingers curl and find that spot inside me that makes my vision blur, and when he sucks on my clit harder, my orgasm hits. Spikes of delight ping up and down my body, and I'm lost in a sea of bliss as he licks and sucks me.

I'm still buzzing with the aftermath of pleasure as they gentle their touches.

"Beautiful," Jason says, brushing hair from my face.

Devon kisses my inner thigh before sitting up. "Always is."

I lie back, boneless, catching my breath as Jason says, "My turn to taste you," and nudges Devon aside.

I whimper as Jason's mouth replaces Devon's. Just as when he and Devon were chopping wood, Jason's technique is different but equally skilled. Where Devon knows exactly what I like, Jason explores, trying different strokes until he finds things that make me gasp.

"Finger fuck her at the same time. That really gets her going," Devon says as he pulls on my nipples and watches the pleasure on my face.

Jason hums in acknowledgment, sliding two thick digits inside me as his tongue continues its work. The combination has me arching off the couch again, oversensitive from my first orgasm and building toward a second.

"Too much? Should I stop?" Jason asks, pausing briefly.

"Don't you dare."

His voice vibrates against my pussy. "Yes ma'am."

Devon has his cock out of his sweatpants and he's stroking it as he watches me. "She gets bossy when she's desperate."

"I noticed," Jason replies, and suddenly he finds that perfect spot inside me. The bliss is so intense, I cry out as he massages the pleasure point, and he laughs joyfully at my reaction as he keeps working his fingers in the same rhythm.

The second orgasm crashes through me faster than the first, my pussy clenching as delight washes over me. He fucks me through it, his pace slowing as I come down from the peak.

"Fuck," I breathe, collapsing back against the cushions. "You two are going to kill me."

"What a way to go," Devon says, leaning down to kiss me.

When he ends the kiss, Jason sits on my other side and tilts my face toward him. My wetness glistens on his mouth, and my pulse jumps the instant I taste myself on his lips. The deliciously dirty rush hits hard.

"I want to see her ride you," Devon tells Jason, his voice rough with arousal.

Jason's eyes meet mine, a question in them. I nod and straddle him as he pulls his cock out of his sweatpants. I'm slick from two orgasms and he slides into me smoothly.

"Fuck, that's hot," Devon says, watching where our bodies are joined as I sit up straight in Jason's lap and rotate my hips.

"Touch yourself," I tell my husband. "I want to watch."

He pulls his cock out without hesitation and wraps his palm around his shaft. He strokes himself in time with my rocking on Jason's cock. I love knowing both men will do anything to please me. I didn't expect that when Devon talked about us inviting Jason to join us, so it's a very welcome benefit.

"Now stick it in my mouth," I demand, and Devon kneels on the couch next to me.

The angle is awkward but workable, allowing me to take him between my lips as I continue riding Jason. The taste of my husband's cock in my mouth while I'm grinding down on his best friend is the perfect kind of dirty for me.

"Fuuuuck," Devon says as I hollow my cheeks around him. "You're blowing my mind, baby."

Heh, while I blow him. But my mouth is too busy to make the joke. Jason grasps my hips and forces me to bounce on his cock.

"She's getting close again," Jason observes, his thumb finding my clit. "I can feel her tightening."

Devon's hands are on my head to guide me, his thrusts careful despite his obvious arousal. "That makes two of us."

The build toward my third orgasm is more intense, and I can tell it's going to be massive when it hits. My toes curl as Jason continues to rub my clit while I suck on Devon. I'm just a little fucktoy for them, but I chose this. I'm the conductor and the orchestra, and knowing I'm in control of our pleasure sends me over the edge.

I'm trembling in delight as I go wild, pounding down on Jason and sucking harder on Devon's cock. I want to pull them with me and when they groan, I know it's working.

"Such a good little slut," Devon growls as he explodes in my mouth.

His words trigger another cascade of bliss. I scream around Devon's cock as pure joy zips from my head to my toes. Jason follows immediately, and a shiver wracks his body as he pumps hot cum inside me.

For one perfect moment, we're caught up in the ecstasy as we writhe together, each of us chasing the high.

My brain is fuzzy by the time we slow down, and when Devon pulls his cock out of my mouth, cum and saliva drips down my chin. I giggle as I wipe it off with my fingers and then lick them clean.

Devon sits down on the couch, and I climb off Jason and collapse into Devon's lap.

"Holy shit," I manage, my voice muffled against Devon's skin.

"Yeah," Jason agrees, his head tipped back against the cushions.

"That was..." Devon starts, then laughs. "I don't even have words."

I lift my head, looking between them with a satisfaction that borders on smugness. "You two make pretty good fucktoys."

They both laugh, and I giggle with them.

I settle deeper into Devon's lap, completely content.

"Give me a minute," I say. "Then we can start round five."

Their synchronized groans of mock protest warm my heart. My first-time hotwife experience has turned out better than I ever imagined.

CHAPTER 5

The next day, Devon and I stand on the porch waving goodbye as Jason pulls out of the driveway. Devon's arm is around my waist and to any observer, we'd look like we were seeing off a casual visitor—not the man who spent two days helping to rock my world.

"Well, this was an interesting weekend," I say, leaning against Devon.

He raises an eyebrow. "Interesting? That's what you're going with?"

"Eh, it was all right." I shrug playfully.

"All right?" His voice drops to a growl as he turns, backing me against the outside wall of the house. "You're about to get more than all right, baby."

His mouth crashes onto mine, hungry and possessive. I moan into the kiss, instantly wet. He pins my wrists above my head firmly.

"Admit it," he demands. "This weekend was fucking incredible."

I smirk, wrapping a leg around his waist. "Make me."

He grinds his cock against me through our clothes. "You want to play it like that? Fine."

He trails kisses down my neck. My breath catches as his hand slides under my shirt to cup my breast, thumb brushing over my hard nipple.

"Come on, Kristy," he coaxes, voice low. "Tell me how great it was. Tell me how much you loved fucking us."

I'm not ready to give in yet, so I bite my lip, fighting a smile. "It was tolerable."

Devon slips his fingers into my shorts, finding my clit. I jolt at the contact, pleasure sparking through me.

"You sure it was just tolerable?" he asks, circling slowly. "If you don't like what we did, I should probably just stop what I'm doing right now."

I squirm against his hand. "Okay, okay," I gasp. "Yes, it was fucking incredible, it was amazing, are you happy now?"

"Getting there," he says smugly, continuing those maddening circles. "Now tell me you want to do it again."

Pleasure simmers in my core and my thighs quiver. "Again? You think you can handle it?"

He rests his forehead against mine. "I think we both know I can. The question is, can you?"

I laugh, breathless, and it turns into a moan when he slides two fingers into my pussy. "God, yes. I want to do it again. I want to make this a yearly thing. Invite Jason back every spring."

Devon's eyes light up. "Sounds good to me."

He kisses me, swallowing my moans as his hand speed up. I can't think when he stops rubbing me and yanks my shorts down in one fluid motion. His cock springs free as he shoves his sweatpants low, then he hooks my thigh over his hip and thrusts deep, shoving my back against the house.

I immediately detonate and cry out as bliss wracks my body. He fucks me roughly, pounding into me, and all I can do is hang on and take it.

He groans, "Fuck, I love you," as pleasure ripples through his body and he blows his load.

Another orgasm hits. It's a soul-shaking orgasm I wasn't expecting, and I can't breathe. I cling to his shoulders as my knees go weak. He continues to fuck me and doesn't stop until I whimper.

"Next summer it is," he agrees. "But for now, you're all mine."

I smile, wrapping my arms around his neck. "Always yours. And by next summer I'll be ready for two cocks again."

"Hell, I'm going to need a year to recover," he says as he pulls his pants up and lifts me into his arms.

He carries me inside, leaving my shorts on the front stoop. I giggle at the absurdity and utter rightness of it all.

When Devon sits down on the couch with me in his lap, I wiggle against his cock.

He grins. "I think you're insatiable."

"And you love it."

"I do," he agrees, expression softening. "I love you."

After everything we've shared this weekend, the simple words fill me with warmth. "I love you too."

His finger traces my cheek. "Was this good for you?"

"Definitely," I assure him. "You?"

"Mmm, yeah, and now I wish I had suggested this sooner."

I snuggle against him. "Now look who's the insatiable one."

We have one more day at the lake house, and I want to spend our last night enjoying this wonderful connection with my husband.

Even though we're leaving the lake soon, this new chapter of our marriage is just beginning. And I can't fucking wait to see what happens next.

Here we observe the thoroughly satisfied suburban wife, already planning her next adventure while thoroughly enjoying the current one.

The End

ABOUT LACEY CROSS

Lacey Cross is a wife sharing erotica writer with over 100 short stories published since she started in 2021. Her stories emphasize the pleasure found from the wife living her best slut life and embracing the hotwife lifestyle. She explores themes of free use, submissive wives with dominant bulls, BDSM...and oh-so-many men.